ADVENTURE

CLASSICS

ADVENTURE
CLASSICS

Tom Sawyer
Out of Time

Wilson Toney

WONDER MILL
COSMOS

wondermillcosmos.com
adventureclassicsbooks.com

With apologies to Langhorne

Preface

This story begins at the end of *Tom Sawyer Abroad*. If you haven't read it, shame on you.

1

In the Cave

Jim had left to get the pipe and Tom and I was just sitting down to discuss things whilts Jim was gone. We of course discussed the usual things of why in the hell we decided to go abroad in the first place when Missouri had mor'n nuff stuff for any man, how long it would take Jim to get the pipe as I was really craving some tabbcy, and how rich we'uns would be one day (Tom thought of this of course). But even these exciting topics only take so long and then we kinda settled down to stare at each other, which, given that neither one of us was all that pretty to start with sure grew tiresome.

Tom was the first (weren't he always though) to

start to philosophizing about this that the other, general stuff that none of us really liked to admit we thought about being half barbarians that we thought we were, regardless of the civilizing done by them that thought they were our betters.

"You know," Tom said, likely knowing that I didn't, "I have heard that people in this here part of the world don't rightly believe in God. At least not in the God that we knows and that loves us in spite of us being half barbarians and all."

As I said, he knowed I didn't know but that's Tom ways, to act like I'm half as smart and half as educated as he is, knowing full well, on my best days I can read maybe my name if someone has writ it real pretty.

"Well, folks is different," I said, as if I was as worldly as the next. "Not everyone believes that Missouri is the best damn place to live, including us evidently or else we wouldn't be in this God Forsaken cave."

"Well there is taste," Tom admitted, staring not so much as me as through me as is often his way, "But then there is logic. How anyone can think that God is different for different folks is beyond even an educated man like me to understand. After all, they's only one world, unless someone is keeping a big secret from us, and we all live in that world. Why would there be different' gods, running all over the place. I suppose God would put an end to that in a hurry being that there ain't but one of him. But it still is hard to believe that people don't believe alike."

Now I ain't one to ruin a good conversation by putting in any logic, specially when I don't know logic from a horse's back side but it did occur to me and I said before thinking, "Where there's one of things they's often more than one of things. "

Tom being educated, and more churchified to boot than me, replied, "That's true about earth things but God ain't no earth thing, and they's only one of him, least the Methodists so believe and that likely makes it so, as the Methodists tend to run things most places. They's smarter I recon than Baptists, although I've heard it say by some that the Presbyterians run some places in Missouri."

I really had to bite my tounge on that, for having only a little bit of Pentecostal churching myself, it was hard for me to think a Presbyterian could run anything, but Tom knows mor'n me and likely he was right.

I wanted to change the subject, I really wanted Tom to start staring through me, as it was spooky even when coming from your best friend. "Tom, usen's are barbarians and don't hold with no churchifying anyway, why don't we talk about plunder and other things useful rather than pretending we know somthin we don't have a clue about."

"They is wisdom in that, " Tom admitted, and we of course continued to talk about churchifying things anyway.

"They say," Tom said, which was likely the they to start with, "That in some cities thy have nye on 50 religions, at least in the north, course, you don't expect much from Yankees no how but seems to me that 50 religions thinking they all have a different God, would be bad for the churchifying business and people would likely get confused on the subject, and possibly give it up as too confusing ."

That'us Tom for you, if they's away to think about how to make a business out of something he would think of it. It must be a wonder to have such a mind, and a good reason to keep him as a best friend as he would likely need help when he was running half of Missouri, and I don't mind admitting my prospects of employment would not be any to great left to their own devices.

After a time even the most lofty idees get tiresome to talk about so, Tom and me, drifted on into discussions on why God made Yankees, and particularly Girls and other distasteful subjects then we gave it up as too deep for the understanding of barbarians, even a well educated barbarian like Tom.

"You know Huck," Tom said, again knowing I wouldn't know, "Have you ever wondered why God made time?'

Now even though Tom was as well educated as a barbarian could be, this was a dasn't subject that the Pentecostals had drilled into me, even given what little time I was in their Church. God don't like nobody discussing time, and why something happened and who it happened to and all such of other deviltry. We is after all, his children, and he knows what's best for us, even if it turns out to be gored by oh Molly the usual gentlest of those to be milked on a Tuesday.

"I'se got to admit Tom," I had to admit, "I ain't thought nothing bout no time, and about no predestination and about how we ain't got a choice in life, even though we have a choice but God knows what choice we is gong to make. Life is to dear to me to muddle up what little thinking ability I has, with stuff even preachers can't figure out, and them being able to read not only they's name but the Bible."

"I ain't talking about no Sunday go to meeting time," Tom said and then muddled up the conversation even more, "I mean everyday, the clock ticks off and another day comes and you can't go back but you can go forward. No other thing allows you to only do one thing. You can fill a bucket and empty it, you can walk frontards or backards, you can"

I stopped him right there because what he was saying was nonsense, "Tom they's lots of things you can only do one way, you can't spit and then unspit. The tabaccky's gone onct it leaves your mouth."

"Yeah but that's cause it's all wound up with time, Huck," Tom said, with a look of knowing something I didn't in his eyes, which he likely did. "If you choose to unspit, you can swaller," Tom said, "That's what I mean, but once you spit or swaller, time has done taking over and you can't undo it."

"Ain't that the same as walking backards or forwards? Once you walk backards, you has done walked backards and you can't undo that neither." I protested

"Well, that is a point, but a very secondary one to the main thesis," Tom said, and I didn't know what no thesis was, but from the tone of his voice, I thought I heard that I had won what little argument there might have been about the subject so I was satisfied.

"I got some thinkin to do on time," Tom said, and that pretty much ended the conversation. He quit staring through me, and started staring at the blank walls of the cave. That was alright by me, but, during our speechifying, we had neglected to stoke and refresh the fire and as night was setting on, it was getting right cold, so I left Tom to his thinking, and I went outside and gathered some dead branches from some strange looking trees (they'd be thought of as shrubs in Missouri, these furriners don't even know how to get trees to grow proper) and when I got back Tom was sound asleep. I joined him soon enough, but I was chased in my dreams by a giant clock asking me why I wanted to unspit in the first place that night and when I woke I figured God was telling me to stop all the nonsense and quit ackting like I was anything but a barbarian.

2

In the Marketplace

There is this to be said about doing nuttin, it takes a lot of doing after a spell. After all, you can talk, and you can talk, and you can talk, but after a shorter time than you consider proper the talking ain't being heard and you shore ain't hearing the other talk, so natural like, when this occurs, you decide it's time to do something.

Doin something, is the easiest thing in the world in Missouri, you can, go catch crawdads for fun or for eats, depending on your particular needs, see if you can swipe an apple or pear from Old Purdy's orchard, but that's mostly a night time affair and even then dangerous ,as she is some shot with her rock salt loaded shotgun, or do some other worthy endeavor that involves irritatin do gooders, but doin something in this here Eygptian place requires really some doin. While we was thinkin on doin something, because it looked like we could have some major doin nothin time, Tom started to think again. Now there ain't much in this world that makes me marvel so much as Tom thinkin, cause he can right do that thing.

"You know, Huck," Tom said, as he picked up a stick and start to poke the ashes, possibly looking for some hidden gold that someone might have just left in our fire pit, "We are in Egypt, and while Egypt don't seem to know a whole lot about the Lord, having no conception of what is fittin for a real God, they do have things like big old burial places called pyramids or somein, and they's probly a mummy or two waiting to be carted off. We could do some business in Hannibal, given we had a mummy to exhibit. Likely we wouldn't want for an apple or tobaccy for a long time, given the goin price on circus exhibits."

Now Tom was talkin, they ain't nothing I like better than the thout of free tobaccky. Why the damn cheap stuff cost now on a penny a plug. Life's luxuries are hard for a poor man to get aholdt of.

"There's lots to that thought Tom," I responded. "If we can get down from this here Mount Sini, I don't doubt that we could find a mummy are two and they would bring some fetching money for exhibition, not to say the chances of swapping to some show boat. They say's they pay up to twenty dollars for a two headed turtle, and them ain't all that hard to find, as I've seen one or two my self," which was a stretch of the truth havin never seen even one except in an exhibit, but I thought it might make Tom even more anxious to find a mummy given he could figure morn' one way of makin money offen it.

"You got a pretty good brain there Huck," Tom agreed. "Let us leave Jim a note that we can be found in the city Reprehenisble, and we shall depart."

Now Tom knowed the name wasn't reprehensible but danged if either of us could figure what to call it from the map we had, and reprehensible it probably was since it was a furrin city, that don't know nothing about Missouri ways, and proper speakin'. Tom also knowed that Jim couldn't even read his name much less a note about a reprehensible city, but that's okay cause Jim didn't want to appear to ignorant so he claimed he could read and Tom dutiifly left a note, but we agreed to draw an arrow towards the city, and Jim could find us there even he ever did find that blasted pipe and just in case he couldn't read. I will say this, if tabaccky warn't good for a sole, I'd plumb give it up as being too hard a pleasure to maintain.

Now reprehensible was some distance away from Mt Sini, and us being not just barbarians but smart barbarians, we aimed to figure aways there that didn't count on us logging too many miles afoot. A man, can always think his way around hard work, particular if that man is Tom Saywer, or at least a man can try.

"The Bible, being the book that it is, is long on descriptions of what to do and pretty short on how to get places," Tom lamented. "Seems to me, they'd done some better by including a paragraph or two on the bestes way to get down from Mount Sanai without having to cling to a perch like a blasted monkey as you descend, seems to me they shoulda said, to get off Mount Sanai, go north a bit and hit the road downwards."

"Well, " I replied, "it does seem the writers of the Bible warn't as practical a person as you is no how, as they's more concerned about the living forever and what not, rather than getting to a place easily. But then, practical people do tend to live a more comfortable life even if they looses to the devil in the end." If there was any comfort in that statement to Tom, he didn't let on, but then again, I've seen books easier to read than Tom when he don't want to let on, and this from a guy that can't read a lick.

Since Jim done took our balloon when he went to get my pipe, it was obvious we couldn't use it, and since we didn't have no way to no road, even if the Bible had told us about said road, we couldn't get down that away. Finally, we decided the only way down was to rope it over, like we used to do in Missouri, even if we did skin ourselves aplenty, like we had moren't oncet when trying rope over in them good old days.

Now rope over aint' that hard, if you got a true set

engineering mind, which Tom allowed he had, after all he was going to be a captain on a Wheel turner one day and that called for engineering aplenty. But still each engineering challenge had it 'a skill set and Tom had never been the tier on the rope over so he didn't know how to make a slip knot that held going down but slipped when tugged correctly, which is the only way for rope over to work, un less you intends to leave your rope behind. However, I showed Tom how to do it, and didn't let on that I thought him any less an engineer because he didn't know how, though it did set my mind to some doubt.

So we roped over on down Mt Sini and after a natural piece of time found ourselves at the bottom, where thankfully we could see a road that headed toward Reprehenisble. They was also a man headed to Reprehensible that looked like he wouldn't know if abody snuck aboard his wagon, as it was long wagon , and it was filled with corn (which them ignorant furrienrs call emmer) and we comfortably slipped underneath. Now corn, is good to eat, and corn pays lots' of bills for lots of people so I don't like to speak badly about it, but it is hot and itches to high heaven, so I privately had bad thoughts about it, even if we didn't want to be kicked out and have to walk to Reprehenisble, or even worse, have to pay for the privlidge of hiding in the corn to get therto.

Finally Reprehenisble was upon us, and we snuck out of the corn as quickly and easily as if we was doing it back in Missouri, which is no reason to think it wasn't something to accomplish, just cause we had experience doing it before. Doubtless a Missouri farmer would be harder to trick, as I doubted the Egyptians were on to Missouri tricks, but you never knows, as boy barbarians anywhere tend to do about the same things if left to be boy babarians.

I have been to few cities it is true, and most of them cities was only water cities off the Missisip, but still, there was nothing stranger in the whole wide world than Reprehenisble. Why those furriners didn't know no better than to build houses out of mud, can you imagine? Course, when I mentioned this to Tom, he was imperlight engought to point out "They ain't no trees about, how you gona build a house outa wood with no trees?"

"Tom, you has got a point, but still, building outa mud something that outa be buildt out a trees, might be one reason not to build here to start with," and even the great Tom Sawyer allowed that was a good reason to suspect the logic of furriners.

Reprehenisble was likely bigger'n Hannibal, as we noted when we flew over it in our balloon, but it ain't noways as pretty as Hannibal. They's don't believe in flowers and such, since they ain't got a river that runs by, just some ocean or another that probably don't hold a candle to the missisip, and thus they use rocks as play pretties aobut there yards. If you can think of anyting uglier than a mud house and a yard full of colored rocks then you is a better thinker than me, but at least Reprehensible did have a market.

Now furriners have their ways, no doubt, but a market is a market, and every man that goes to a market thinks he's gonna skin the other guy in trade. It often happens that after a trade both guys crow about how they skint the other fellow. This don't make sense, but then, not all things do make sense that happen, but they happen anyway.

So there was the biggest bunch of stalls, and wagons selling stuff that you wouldn't likely need in a hurry, such as a branch from the Burning Bush and the Toe Nails of Kind David as well as some stuff that might come in handy, like vegetables, and sheep, and what not. There must have been nigh on to a hundred and fifty of them stalls and wagons and we weren't having nearly enouh time to cover them going together so Tom shoved off separate from me, and said, "Don't get took by these heatherns and I'll see you later." Tom didn't seem to have a lot of confidence in my ability to snooker the next guy, but then, Tom was always besting me so he may have some reason for that viewpoint, but we still went our separate ways, and I didn't aim to let Tom down so I just walked from booth to booth and kept my mouth shut.

Now, Reprehensible is a city that is near the sea, and when you have a sea, you got people from other places arriving by boat and ship and such, and there were plenty of those kinda folks wandering around Reprehensible. Some was obvious reglar people like

Tom and me as they didn't wear no funny headdress, and wore pants instead of skirts like the furriners. Now one of these reglar fellows must have knowed what was what in the selling of things cause he had his on booth and was selling all sorts of useful things, like frogs, and grasshoppers, and other critters, that would be useful in putting down the backs of some no good, so I walked on over to his booth to see what else he had in store.

"Begorra," he said, when I walked, up, and I supposed that was hello in this heathern place so I answered "Begorra yourself." That caused him to smile and that smile showed me he was a man of some means, since he was only missing three teeth and he was at least thirty years of age.

"Begorra is what an Irishman says when they see something oncommon and ain't to be confused with hello," the tradesman replied, now I didn't quite know how to take that as I am about as common as any man can be, but from the way he said it, I didn't think he meant to insult me.

"That asides," the tradesman continued, "What can I do for you young Master?" and again he flashed he smile, which was something to think on, cause a man trying to beat you always smiles to much.

" I was thinking about buying one of your frogs," I said, "As I am a long way from my pet frog in Missou and I long for some pet to make over and eventually to put down somebody's back when they ain't a looking."

"Well frogs are good for that sort of thing, laddie," the tradesman said, or at least I think that's what he said, as it cam out sounding like this, "Welll frugs be goode for some sort of deviltry, laddie," which to be honest with you, put me right off frogs right away. It is one thing to use a frog for it's God intended purpose of scaring the hell out of some no good, interfering with whatever your rightful business was at that time, but getting the devil involved was too much for me. I was on shaky enough ground as it was having thought about predestined or not.

So I says, "Well, don't want no devil frogs," and as I stared to wander off the tradesman proclaimed, "Ye be a man of God then," which again he said as a compliment though I' have known of fights to break out when one boy calls another preacher, when they's disagree on some sort of mischief that involved takin a risk a Preacher might disapprove.

"I don't know if the good Lord would acknowledge me," I admitted, "but I reckon I ain't no worse than most when it comes to thanking him." Now I held my breath just a second, as I've been told, when you tell a whopper on God, he's apt to put lighting through you, but after a second or two passed, and nothing struck me, I figured God was either to busy to care, or I was so fer gone that he didn't want to wast the time killing me and just doing the Devil a favor by delivering me early. "That be wisdom laddie," the tradesmen said, "And I got something that you will like give to your Church and the Priest that has done well by you." Now I ain't no redneck and I know people use words different in different places, but this seemed pretty high faluting to call a Preacher a Priest, just cause they Bible says they were Preists in them good old days. Next he would be referring to them as ministers or reverends or some other sort of fancy word. Don't know why people have to put on airs.

"I don't reckon I like my Preacher or Church enugh to give em anything," I said, "Cause likely they's already got it and it's better than anything I could afford to give em," it's best to come off as rather poorly anytime there is a potential negotiation, so as not to give the other fellow any ammunition in case it preceeds beyond the discussing stage and into the dickering stage

"Come now my young Sir and look at this one of a kind Holy object, passed down from father to son for millinia, and came into my hands through only the most fortunate of circumstances," the Irish man tried to say, though what I heard was "Come now youn sucker and get ye took but good."

I came there, even though it was agin my better judgment as I ain't ashamed to admit, I done been took in deal making more that I have taken, but the palaver was a wonder to behold, and if nuttin else, I wanted to hear more of the man's tounge than I expected any sort of real item to purchase.

As I approached closer, the tradesman smiled that winning smile and reached under his table for somein. Having had negotiations similar before, I expected it would be a plain old snake that he was gonna try to convince me was a copper head (I've even seen the trick tried using a common snake for a rattler to, but you gotta be uncommon stupid to mistake any other snake for a rattler), but instead he came out with a piece of paper in his hand that looked like it had seen better days.

"Let us endeavor to evaluate this beauty," the tradesman said, which I guess was his words for let's make medicine. Well I evaluated that beauty all right, and for sure I couldn't make head nor tail of it. It was an old brown piece of paper, that had some sort of numbers and writing on it. I of course knows my numbers (at least I claims to although after the first round of em, I gets kinda confused, and am just as likely to make a deal thinking I'm gonna get 31 of some'n and wind up with 13 as not) but these were well behaved numbers and only started at 1 and goes to 10. The writing on em meant nuttin to me, but I didn't let on, cause, usually them that don't pretend to know morn' they do gets beat in a deal affore it starts.

"That is right pretty," I agreed, "But the paper is beginning to look the worset of it, you might want to think on getting a Preacher or School Marm to rewrite that thing on something fresh."

I thought the tradesman was gonna faint on the spot. "Young Master, none of it, why do you know this is none other than the original ten commandments, written by Moses himself upon his descent from the mountain after communing with the good Lord"

Well now, that gots me to thinking. Everybody's heard of Moses of course, and everybody had heard of the ten commandments, and there would be some trading for sure, if I could get aholdt of that document and take it back to Hannibal with me. Course I didn't let on that I thought it was anything special, as I wanted to try to get the better of the deal. "Well," I lied, "I has seen others about selling them ten commandments so the price has got to be about right or I wouldn't be interested." Still it sounded like some pedigree, and I was ready to fork over a few good old gold coins to obtain it.

"You ain't seen nobody sell them ten commandments," came Tom Sawyer's voice. He had evidently overheard us talking and decided to interject himself into this hoss trade. Now I knows Tom better'n most, and I know he wouldn't be giv'n the other guy any ammo to use agin me, but I couldn't rightly see how anyone thought that letting the guy think he had the only one of something gives you any leverage in the proceedings.

"How's that Tom?" I asked, hoping he would rethink and say he was mistaken and he had seen seventy-eleven of them documents floating about.

"As I noticed, right off," Tom continued, with that air he gets when he has done outsmarted someone, "Those Ten Commandments are written in English.

I doubt that Moses, man o God though he was, ever learn't English before the English people invented it."

Well the tradesman heard that and was fit to be tied, and he was likely gonna come back with another stretcher or two, just so he could say he tried, but Tom just nodded his head at me and we went for greener, or at least, less imaginative, pastures.

We continued on through the market and I gotta tell you, them furriners have their funny ways. They was men dressed as women, but you could see their face, and their was women dressed as women but you couldn't see hide nor hair of em. Tom called them burkes or some such, I just thought, they was too lazy to fix themselves up for the general public, so they just hid underneath a blanket an called it a day.

Tom of course, knew why they did it, "Their religion," Tom stated, "Says that the only man that can look at a woman is her husband. That's why they wear them burka's, so that they don't tempt common folk like you and I".

Well, holding to one's religion I suppose is just as good as not, but still, the thought had occurred that if any of these women looked like ol Maw Purdy, they might just be doing us a real favor, even if they didn't do it for that reason. Most religons' I suspect, have their good parts, regardless of whether you wind up in Heaven or Hell by believing in em.

As I said before, but I repeats because our story is

about to turn on such, they was several reglar people around. Some of them dressed similar to me and Tom, but some was dressed in high falutin clothes that you only see on the ladies of Hannibal when they is going to Sunday go to meeting. One of them dressed high falutin, was a man about mid thirties that wore what looked more like a uniform than like real clothes. He was covered all over in sold white cotton and with a funny white hat on his head, that would have been a fair target for most of us boys if we saw him walking the streets of Hannibal.

Now I weren't totally convinced that Tom was rite about them ten commandments, but I was hesitant to challenge him, he being Tom and all, but once I heard that man in white speak, I knew I had some-one to ask. The man talked with the dangest tones, good old English but the English was like what you hear on the showboats that come about ever so often and have shows about people you never heard of like Hamlet or Mcbath. The man in white was using just them tones to try to dicker down an Ayerab that was aholdt of a piece of pottery that woulda been thrown out of the house in Hannibal, it looking so old and broken, even by a man as cheap as my daddy.

I ain't typically so bold, but I had a hankering for them commandments if they'us real, cause I could sure see some people in Hannibal that might be willing to give even six months worth of tabacky for it, just to show they was serious about the Lord and all, that I decided to go up and ask the man if the ten commandments was writ in English at the first. I hated to think anything Tom said didn't make sense, but after all the Bible was writ in English, even I knew that.

So I eases up to the man and kinda let him catch on that I's there then I says, when he glances at me kinda irritated, "Is yen's an English feller?"

Right off he gave me the evil eye, which to yeens that don't know, is when someone looks at ye and sees some sort of varmint to be run offt, but him being English, he was also to polite to tell me to go on about my business as he had none with me and he says, "Yes I am jolly well English"?

Why anybody thouth it was a fun being one thing rather than another I didn't know, cause I was proud to be an American, but I warn't particular jolly over it, but I let it pass as that kinda superior way of talking that some gets when they thinks they's speaking to their lessers.

"Well, Mr. Englishman," I says, "I am Huck Finn and this ere's Tom Sawyer," I says and nods to my friend Tom as I was saying it, but Tom didn't look like he was any to happy over this happening, and he would likely be less happy when he heard my question.

"Glad to meet you, I'm sure," the Englishman sad, though I couldn't detect no particular delight in his voice over the prospect, and then he turned away to start hammering at the Ayerab again.

"Mr Englishman," I continued, in as uppity a

voice as I could master as I was likely talking to gentily here, or at least gentily as seen by some, I didn't rightly know what the word meant but a store of women in Hannibal sure put great stock by it, and this rigid Englishman with a funny hat seemed more gentle than most I come in contact with, "I just wanted to know if you knew what the ten commandments was written in. Tom thinks, it weren't English, but if so, I just wanted to make sure an Englishman agrees, cause if you don't I got some dickering to do."

"Master Tom, is correct," the Englishman stated, "The original ten commandments was likely in Hebrew, and then was translated into Greek and then translated into English." With that, the man in white turned from me and lost all interest.

Well I was a mite disappointed, and I thought about going back and dickering with the Irish man anyway, but it was a sure thing that if even Tom knew it was fake most wealthy and educated people would know it was a fake. Since I's unlikely to take any wealthy man to the cleaners during a trade, and poor folk like me wouldn't have anything to trade anyway, I gave it up as one more tempatation that I had resisted to take advantage of folks, and hope the Lord took it the same way, though if he could see into my heart as some says, he'd know I's just giving it up because it wasn't a scheme likely to bring any return for my efforts.

"Let's be off Huck," Tom said, kinda sad like, as

if I had hurt him some in questioning his judgment, thoe I wouldn't hurt Tom for the world, I might for 6 months of tabacky, but I just nodded and walked away with Tom.

We hadn't gone mor'n two feet when Tom says real excited, "That woman in the burka's got a gun!"

Now I of course looked about for some woman in a burkes, and let me tell you that was plenty of them about, but not many had guns out, when I saw a flash of light agin somthin and my glance naturally went that away. Sure enuf, there was a lady in a burkes with a long, thin object that sure resembled some sort or rifle, thow not one I'se familiar with, but then Hannibal was known for a lot of things, but being the first to get a new type gun aint' one of them.

The lady with the rifle was pointing the gun dead straight at the English feller with the funny hat and Tom saw it right away. He screamed "Get Down English Feller!!!" at the top of his lungs and flung himself at the lady, which might not be as polite as some would allow, still aiming a gun ain't so lady like either, and perhaps that was a mitigation.

Tom hit the woman just as she seemed to pull the trigger on that rifle, and the shot went astray and instead of taking out the white hatted English feller it done the vase he was looking at for keeps, which was probly a blessing as at least the English feller wouldn't get took in the purchase. As Tom piled on, I came in just behind, swinging the right hook that had once takin down that braggert Jimmy Nolan, thow hear him to tell it he just stumbled at that moment, and it landed fair solid against the lady's nose, and landed hard enough to clear knock the top off that berkes.

There was a sight to behold, when you saw that lady without no covering. Even Ma Purdy would have been easier on the eyes. Course, after a second, I realized it twern't no lady at all but some egg sucking man that had pretended to be a woman, like as not to take advantage of the situation. A meaner man was never to be seen either, with eyes that looked like they had been stolen from Lucifer, and sunken cheeks that needed a good chaw in them to give them some distinction.

The man started to twist and roll and throw us about so he could get off another shot with that fancy rifle, but Tom out thought him, even thow he didn't out fight him, and hooked the rifle with his feet as he was being tossed about and flung the rifle away from us and towards the English feller. Oncet the man saw that his rifle us closer to the English feller than to him, he gave out with a screech and then he hit Tom and me a time or three, then throwed Tom about ten feet. He only managed to throw me about eight feet as I outweight Tom a bit and I was second in line for this particular privelidge, then he took to his heels, like he'd been caught in the watermelon patch right afore harvest, with no reason for being there, as the English feller was fast approaching and already had that new fangled rifle in his hands.

"There goes a man that wants to git," Tom said and half laughed. I was to busted up to laugh myself but then Tom always finds the funny side of things even when they ain't all that funny. I was just thankful to see him go and for some reason I wasn't thinking no more.

3

The Hunter

I supposed I had the vapors or somin, as I sure
didn't know no whole lot for a while, and when I
did know somin I would have just about not known
it. The evil man had left me with a whopper of a
black eye and a knot on my skull, and I felt worse
then anytime Daddy had beat me, which was saying
something. But come to I did, and the English feller and Tom was standin above me when I woke up,
and while the English feller looked concern, Tom
warn't no whole lot, as he had seen me just about
any which way that can be seen and I had always
come through the lickin. This time warn't no difference.

The English feller with the Funny white hat, said,
"Thank God, you are alive young Master." Now I
had heard the tradesman call me a master to and

had let it slide, I ain't rich engouh to own nobody and wouldn't want to even if I could because I's can take care of myself thank you kindly.

"I ain't no Master," I replied, "Just a barbarian that thought he was smart, but even if smart, ain't nearly as tough as he outa be."

Tom was having none of that and he jumped right in, "Huck that man's was twice your size and meaner than a mad dog, you done okay for a barbarian", and while I still didn't agree with him, I felt warm all over to know he said it.

"You Gentlemen have saved my life, and I want to thank you, and to apologize for my boorish behavior earlier," the English feller said, and I warn't sure he was talking to me as I've been acused of lots of stuff but being a gentleman ain't never been one of em.

"We were glad to assist," Tom replied, and continued, "What'd the guy dressed like a woman want to kill you for?"

It took a second for that to register with him cause I think the English feller was listening for an English sentence and what he got was good American, but you could see he finally did understand and he answered, "I have no idea. My name is Allan Quatermain and I am just a hunter, of no particular significance in this world, and with no more enemies than most. I am sure there are many people that wouldn't mind if I died, however I do believe that few of them would want to go to any trouble to see me so."

It was obvious I'se gonna have to listen Hard when this Mr. Quatermain talked, cause, it was about as convoluted as any granny knot I had ever seen tied.

"Well, Mr. Quatermain, it is obvious that, your thoughts on the issue aiside, that the man was aiming for you and not for the vase he bagged," Tom said.

"True enough, young lad," Quatermain replied, "And with a rifle like I have never seen. I have been a game hunter for most my life, and I thought I knew every type of rifle or rifle accroutement there was, and yet I can't make head nor tell out of this piece. Let me demonstrate."

Quatermain demonstrated that gun most nicely. He lined up some gourds on a fence post off in the distance, at least a hundred yards, and he begin to pull the trigger and them gourds went pop right off, one after another, and no sound came from the rifle. I thought a Colt revolver was the cat's meow, but it didn't hold a candle to this here rifle and I pity the man that was on the business end of that thing during a battle. I don't want to Blaspheme none, but I doubt if even on Dan'l Boone hisself coulda done better.

"That is some shooting," Tom said, and it indeed was some shooting.

"Thank you my lad, but did you notice there was no retort nor was there any repelling against my shoulder when I used this weapon?" Quatermain asked but he didn't really expect an answer and got none, besides it took me a minute to figure what he was saying, but in good Missou American it was that the rifle didn't make nary a sound and it didn't buck like a mule as it should.

Quatermain held up the rifle and said, "Why it doesn't weigh ten pounds, and there are no bullets necessary, it seems to be shooting compressed air. A man with an army that had a hundred of these could conquer the world!"

Tom allowed that a hundred men with a rifle such as that could do a lot of damage, but I could tell he thought Quatermain was exaggerating just a bit, as likely as not, the whole world would soon get wise to the army of hundred men and just swallerm whole with a rush of soljers.

"And look at this maker's mark," Allan continued, "It is for the Smithe manufacturing firm, in London England. I thought I knew the maker of every rifle that you could find, be the rifle made in England or Siberia, and I have never hear of Smithe Manufacturing."

Well, I didn't rightly know where Siberia was, but I doubt they were shucks on manufacturing rifles, since most of the ones in Missou came from New York or Illinois or some such and we wouldn't likely take second class rifles. That being said, I understood that anybody from England would likely know the best places to buy rifles, and frogs and all sorts of things in that country, after all, anybody from Hannibal could tell you the cheapest place to buy anything at all, particularly the ladies when looking for fancy doodads at the emporium or at the Gen'l Store.

"Enough of me," Quatermain stated, "How come two youths of your obvious lineage come to be in an Egyptian Bazzar?"

I hesitated for a moment, cause I thought we was at a market, but Tom caught on as quick as a rabbit and understood that Bazzar was just a fancy word for market place.

"Huck, Jim and I, started out for London England in a hot air balloon. Some how or the other we wound up on Mount Sainai. As Huck had left his pipe, we asked Jim to head back to Hannibal, Missouri, to retrieve it. We thought we would see the market prior to heading back when Jim gets back."

"Why you boys might never see Jim again, and he was a rouge for leaving you here at the mercy of the elements and with a strange people," Quatermain said. Well, I grant you Jim wasn't as likely as some to handle a balloon all the way back to Hannibal and return, but he wouldn't leave us on purpose and he would die afore he let anything happen to Tom or me, and we'd do the same for him, but of course, Mr. Quatermain didn't know the what's what and who's who of Hannibal, MO so Tom and I just let it pass.

"You boys must come with me to Britain," Quatermain continued, "And I will ensure that the American consulate will have notice of your arrival." Well, since both Tom and I knew that Jim was as likely to wind up in England when he aimed for Mount Sanai, as he was to hit any other place, we agreed to Mr. Quatermain, after we made sure that the people of the Market Place knew that if Jim showed up to tell him we had headed that way. Now furriners are funny people and some of them ain't as good at English as me and Tom, so I can't guarantee that they fully understood, so Tom and me gathered a bunch of rocks and drew another great arrow on the ground pointed towards the way we were headed.

Just to be sure, Tom wrote in great big letters on the ground:

"JIM WE HAS GONE TO LONDON ENGLAND, OR LONDON BRITIAN, WHICHEVER IS RIGHT AS THESE PEOPLE SEEM TO USE ENGLAND AND BRITAN AT RANDOM WHICH CAN BE A MITE CONFUSING FOR THOSE OF US NOT BORN OF BRITAN OR ENGLAND BUT THEY DON'T PAY NO NEVERMIND AND DO IT ANYWAY SO COME GET US WHEN YOU GET HERE"

Tom then signed his name under the writing and asked me to sign to which I replied, "You sign for me Tom as you have a better way with words than me," which was true but even Tom could tell it was a weak attempt to get around the fact all I could do is make an X and so he signed. Tom has a better way of protecting a man's pride than any other body I have ever met, and of course never let on a whit that he knows. But he knows!

"Now we are set," Tom said, and he and I went to join Mr Quatermain on his ship that was a headed to England we thot, thow we were still a little concerned that it was really Britain and we just had misunderstood. And we were set assuming Jim had learned to read, or the furriners understood what we had said, or the arrow was pointing the right way as we didn't have no map to show us which way England was and we just sorta thought it was pointed the right way or it didn't rain and wash away Tom's writing so Jim could read if he had learned to read while on the balloon. So all things considered, I was satisfied we were set.

4
The Steamship

I am sure the English have their good points same as most people, and whenever you is in a room full of them you can bet they will carry on some about how they's the best at all sorts of things. Being perlite I just nods and agrees, but they ain't got a clue how to build a paddle wheeler.

The steamboat we us on was bigger than a Missisip steamboat, but it couldn't hold a candle to even the worst of em. Why it pitched about worse than a Mexican jumping bean, it had no decent place for boys to sit and watch the Captain work, and not once did he ever mark the depth of the water. What else does a Captain do, if he ain't hollering Mark five or Mark twain or somein. Just goes to show, they's a right way to do things and not everyone gets the message on that way. But being we was Mr.

Quatermain's guests, I made allowances, and didn't mention how badly this steamboat was bein skippered morn fifty or sixty times.

Mr. Quatermain would just smile any time I pointed out some idiotic thing the skipper had just done. Tom would just shake his head, understanding as he did the frustration I had in watching people do something wrong and holding my tounge as best I could about it. All that said, all other things being equal, which they ain't ever but it is a phrase everybody uses, it was a fine trip and Mr. Quatermain even paid for our ways, which was good of him and probably necessary to as I doubt if Tom and me could have gathered mor'n two or three gold coins since ballooning ain't exactly the most prosperous of vocations.

Mr. Quatermain had most of the ship booked for him and hisn. Not to mention me and Huck, he had nigh on 20 others he was paying for. It sure appeared that hunting was better prospects in England than in Hannibal, as every boy in Hannibal and man too hunted and not a one of them could have paid the passage for 20 people on even this second class steamboat. Of the twenty, Mr Quatermain had a half dozen black people with him, but they warn't none of them like Jim and didn't dress they way Jim did, which was mostly better than me and worse than Tom as Tom gave Jim his warn out clothes more often than I got a chance at em.

They was dressed near naked, even though it

weren't always the prettiest site nor likely the warm-
est they could be, with feathers a galore and not
much else, likely as not looking like the Injuns of old
you hear about in Missou but are pretty sure never
really existed cause no one could have it as good as
they. All of them was a lot blacker Jim to and they
all carried spears and looked like they could handle
themselves in any sorta fight and likely would do
better than most.

Now I know, you think I am guilding the goose
here, but it's the truth, they was wearing necklaces
made of teeth and not made of fake pearls like the
ladies at home. They was as handsome as any Injun
you see in a paper book and they weren't no way
shy about it. Like as not they had killed a lion or
tiger or two with their bare hands or else, Mr Quatermain, being the mighty hunter he was, wouldn't
have a need for them.

There were others in Mr. Quatermain's group,
including some Chinamen, even though Mr. Quatermain said they were from Japan, I knows a Chi-
naman when I sees one so I thot they had put one
over on Mr. Quatermain, like as not for higher wag-
es as it was likely Chinamen wouldn't bring as much
in the market being as there was so many of them,
but I never let on, cause they was just working folks
like me and likely needed ever edge they could get.

The most outstanding person that worked for Mr.
Quatermain was Utumbo, who while not the biggest of the Africans, was likely the top dog, as he

dressed just a bit different than the rest, using different colored feathers, not a lot different but enuf to
notice and that was likely the point. Utumbo could
speak a bit of English, and speak it better Mr. Quatermain if you ask me, as he would say strait out,
"Stop that Tom and Huck," when we was up to mischief, whereas Mr. Quatermain would say "Young
Gentlemen that is hardly the way one would con-
duct oneself now is it," or some other statement that
wouldn't exactly roll off the tounge. But Tom and
I understood, and we wouldn't do our mischief in
front of him. We would still do it of course, but we
would act as innercent as you please when it came
to light, and that would fool Mr. Quatermain, but
Utumbo would just bop us and say, "Stop that Tom
and Huck," which is not exactly justice in Hannibal
as they was others you could blame but likely was
justice on the steamboat as the only ones that were
up to anything was me and Tom.

5
Spies

There's always things to do in Hannibal that makes the time pass pretty as you please, if nothing else, skulking about and looking for good hiding places from which to leap out and scare them no good girls, but they's a lot less to do on a second class boat such as Tom and I was floatin on. I means, they's no girls to leap out at and ain't to many places to hide in to make the leap. So time killin took some work, still Tom and me made the best of the siteration.

"Huck," Tom said, "We should know every place of egress on this ship," which didn't mean a whit to me until I follered him around and saw that he meant ways of getting about the boat. So we found all the doors, and all of the passageways, and not an uncommon number of the places yeens could hide and not be seen. This was to serve us in our new occupation as spies, us havin given up ballooning since we didn't have no balloon any more and the pay being so poor and all.

"We should be able to observe every person on this ship," Tom told me with a wink, "And not be seen ourselves. It will make great training for us in our new professions and as the ones that want to hire spies might give us a test, we can be sure to be ready when they ask us to perform."

I don't know nuttin about spying o course, cept that it's right easy to do in Hannibal, as I already knowed every place worth knowing, thow I has to admit, spying was the easy part and earning on the spying was hard. Nobody in Hannibal had every offered me so much as a red cent to tell em I had seen the Preacher walking down main street, even thow he stopped at the Widder Hawkins house when he did walk down main street an stayed over long if you ask me. People just said it was what Preachers do, which is no doubt of some truth, but kissing the Widder Hawkins as you left didn't seem all that Preacherly to me.

Still spying was somein to do and as we was hid while spying, Utumpo couldn't find us and thus couldn't bop us up sides the head. So they's that profit in it even if the money ain't what one would want.

Spying on them soles aboard the ship warn't no great shakes o course, as they didn't try to hide anything's they was doing anyways. I mean who cared if we spied um spitting tabaccky juice or scratching emselves, we alls does them things, and it hardly meant they would pay anything to keep us quite about it. But spies we was, even if it werent' all that glorious after the first few minutes, and spying we did.

We came to know evry man and woman on that boat by site and we had our own nicknames which was descriptive if not the most flattering, like on needle neck for a man that needed to add a pound or two, and Miss Sunday School for a fat old woman that reminded us of our past Sunday School teachers (or at least Tom's, as I can't rightly say I went to any school overly much and that went double for Sunday School) being always in Sunday go to meeting clothes. But we never called them those names in public of course, not wantin to give away the spy trade.

So we would while away an hour or two, spying and talking about Jim and Hannibal and what ye recon happened to such and such and so and so, and it beat doing nutin but not by much. But that changed when we saw a new person.

As we was hid up in a closet looking out over the transom for this particular spying, we was talking about how closet's was the same all over, particular when they contain mops and brooms and such and they all stank, and good thing we was smart barbarians, cause reglar people wouldn't want to be around that stink if they had any sense so no one would look in this closet for us and jus then the new man passed by.

He was tall and thin and had a sunken face and had evil Lucifer eyes and Tom said "Shoosh," and I shoosed and we looked at him walk by. He was dressed in black hat, black jacket, black pants, black shoes, and likely black everything you couldn't see as he looked like that kinder person. I don't know who advised him on sartorial matters but it was a cinch it wasn't no one from Hannibal Mo or else they'd tell him that if you wears black, people will just naterly think you ain't got no color sense and make fun of you behind your back. Course, the people of Hannibal would likely make fun o you behind your back even you wore all red or all white or anything else all, as it warn't the current fashion, but that was another point altogether.

The man took a lightly stroll past us and kept on a going about his business if any, and Tom whispered, "Let's see where that no good is going."

I can't rightly say how Tom knew the guy was no good, as I thought that was quite a leap from a guy wearing all black to being no good, thow wearing all black did show a lack of imagination, it didn't necessarily follow that the guy was a no gooder, but then Tom' has his ways and he is without doubt more right than wrong, sides, the mop smell was a getting to my sensibilities anyway so I's ready for a change.

Tom opens the door slowly, so as not to make

any quick noises, and I'se follers him, and we looked down the hall way just in time to see the man in black turn a corner. We didn't wait any in beating feet that way, knowing that the man might go into any of the rooms to the left or the right, and he might go up on the upper deck or lower deck or he might disappear into thin air and that'd be something to see.

Then we hits the corner on the run then, kinda stopped and Tom cricked his neck round the corner so that his body was still hid by the wall. That's wise, o course, as the man might be waiting to pot shot us, thow why he would I hadn't answered in my on mind, still it was better to be safe than shot, so I respected Tom for stopping and craining.

Tom didn't say nothing but just jerked his head at me and stated on down the hall way. I follered knowing the guy would shoot Tom first and I'd have a chance to beat feet the other way if it came to it. It didn't come to it though as the hallway was plumb empty.

"Did you see him disappear Tom?" I asked, thinking maybe I'd missed some big news by not being as brave as Tom.

"Uh?" Tom asked with a queer look on his face.

"Just thout he might've disappeared in then air as they says," I replied.

"Not into thin air," Tom said and continued to walk, "But into that room," and Tom nodded his head at room 3 B, as we passed. Course we didn't stop. We kep on walking, and looking for spying places, and naturaly the only one we found was another mop and brook closet, which we entered. That closet gave us good view of 3 B, but it lacked just a bit in what I consider aromatic.

"Tom," I whispered, once we had got set amongst the mops and brooms and buckets and such, "Why do you think that man dressed in black is a no good? Outside, he looks ornery and dressed in black like he was an outlaw an all I mean?"

"That's the man that shot at Mr. Quatermain," Tom replied.

Now I allowed that I only had a quick glance at the man that was dressed like a woman and that had a fancy gun, and I also allowed that I was knocked sillier than a ring tailed raccoon when the man hits me, but I just didn't think that man we follered looked like that no good that shot at Mr. Quarermain.

"You shore, Tom?" I asked, as I wanted to be shore we didn't waste any too much spying time in this smelly place lessen we had to.

"Shore enough," Tom replied, "While I admit the face ain't exactly right, any spy can change his face, but the eyes of Lucifer, they're a dead give away."

Well Tom's eyes are bettern' most and while stinky places and the greatest place fer spyin I reconded I could stand it if Tom could, so I just said, "Well, I'll shore stay as long as you will Tom and then some, thow we might want to take turns being it's nigh on supper time and I ain't et since lunch."

"We'll go hungry this night," Tom stated dramatically and with a stern look on his face. Well, I've been hungry moren I ain't benn hungry so it didn't bother me no whole lot, but I gotta admit I didn't see the sense in both of us missing out on the meals.

"Tom," I says, "I'll miss any a meal you will, but I still don't see why we can't take turns."

"Cause we might have to tussle with that no good," Tom replied and I saw his eyes flash when he spoke. "Why we are smart barbarians, ain't neither one of us full grown yet and two hands is bettern' one when there's a fight on."

There was sense to that, but given the fact the no good had about taken my head off the last time we fought, I warn't particularly raring to give it another go. But I'd do what I had to, or else be shamed in Tom's eyes, and I'd rather be dead than that.

Well they was nothing to it but to set down and wait, so we wait, takin turns peering over the transom at the door 3 B. That was as long a wait as I have ever experience what with being afraid we would miss him and being just as afraid we wouldn't miss him, but the time proceeded as it always does, which reminded me of Tom's take on why time didn't go this away and that away and why you can't unspit but can swaller and predestined and…thank God, the no good in 3 B opened the door and walked out so I quit a thinking.

Me and Tom being close to expert spies, havin practiced it for nigh on 6 hours or so, decided the proper time to give the no gooder was ten seconds afore we came out of that mop closet. So we did, and then we got and was glad of it, for the air warn't gitting any sweeter in there. They's should be special pay for spies givn' what we has to do for our jobs.

Tom said, "Act natural," and started walking behind the no good, whistling and casting his eyes left and right, so as not to let on. I follered Tom's example and whistled my on true self and hummed a hymn I had heard oncet in Penecostal church. Well, that no good must a been a Methodist or somn cause quick as he heard me a humming he stopped, turned and gave us the evil eye but good.

Tom and I didn't pay him no never mind o course as a spy ain't supposed to let on. We must have fooled him into thinking we was just there by accident, as he continued walking and turned his head away from us so as not to trip over things. We kinda mosied on after him, not hurrying o course but just enough to keep him covered.

As he headed up on deck we had the misfortune of running into Utumbo while we was a whistling and humming and of course acting natural. Utumbo took one look at me and Tom and said "Tom and Huck stop that," and just immediate bopped me one on the noggin. I will say this, how Utumbo knowed we was doing anything other than acting natural was beyond me, but knows he did.

Tom tried to evil eye Utumbo but it did not good. "Go to room, or go to supper," Utumbo said, "But quit acting stupid,"

That hurt Tom but good, as he don't never act any way but smart and right, course I was acting stupid most the time, so I didn't take no offense at the statement, but Tom and I drifted on away and let the no good man pass from our vision. I of course headed for the kitchen wiched them what done know how to speak called the galley for no good reason, as it seemed supper was now on our list of things to do, but Tom was of sterarner stuff and he grabbed me by the arm as quick as we got out of Utumbo's site and said, "Now's the time to search that no good's cabin."

I warn't overly fond of that thought myself, as I have been caught a time or two in somebody's house when I warn't supposed to be there, and I got a liken by them and then by pap when I got home. Pap didn't care I was in somebody else's house o course, he likked me cause I warn't smart enuf to not get caught.

But regardless of my feelings on the subject, and to be fair to Tom I didn't come right out and say, "Tom you stupid or somen?" but just kinda let my eyes say I wasn't keen on the idee, and subtlety was lost on Tom as we headed, lickety split to the no good's cabin.

Any boy in Hannibal Mo, or likely any other place knows how to open a door when it is locked as long as the idjits put the hinges on the outside. It only takes a team of two, one will jimmy the hinges, the other hold the door, then you enter and reput the hinges on. Which is what I woulda done, but Tom of course, being a spy of much greater smarts says, "We got's to find a way into that Cabin that don't show that No Good how we did it."

Well I hated to mention bout the hinges, Tom being so much smarter than me and all, but then I got to thinking, Tom was a lot more church going than me and as a lot of time that when mischief was committed, since they was less chance o getting caught that way, so Tom might not know. And he didn't but saw it right off when is said, "Tom we can get a pair a plyers and a hammer from that stinky closet and have that door off them hinges quick as a cat. Then you can enter and unlock the door, we can put her back on their hinges, and we can then do as we please and as long as we lock up when we leave, No Good won't have a clue."

Tom saw the wisdom in that right off, sides, they warn't likely any other way into the room, since it only had the one door and the winder opened out into the ocean. Still, it made me some proud to make a contribution to our spyin no matter how small.

It didn't take no morn five minutes to get into the room, and we o course, made special careful not to damage the hinges incase old No Good was sharper eyed than most. Once in, we had to light the lamp, which took a time, cause, I didn't have no matches and neither did Tom, but we was able to light a piece a paper on the lamp outside and put it on to the wick of the lamp inside. They's an oder left when you burned paper o course, but being that most every body smoked roll your owns on board, we hoped that even if no good smelled it, he would pass it off as just a cigarette.

The room once lit, was no different than ours on the inside, but we noticed right off that they was something strange going on. The man had left his suitcase on the floor where any fool would trip over it in the middle of the night, in case he had to get up for some reason, and no lamp on.

"Ain't hardly an experienced traveler," Huck, Tom whispered, "Else that suitcase would be in the closet."

I agreed but didn't say nuttin as it was obvious and sides something else had caught my attention. Lying on that floor just next to the suitcase was the dangest thing I'd ever seen in all my born days. They was a pair a shoes that didn't have no good top, and no good bottom, and had no loop arounds for tying. Tom, saw me looking and he looked to and I gotta say, not much puzzles old Tom, him being the smartest kid in Hannibal, Mo and all, but that did.

Tom reached down and picked up one of them shoes and looked it to the left and to the right then back again. He tossed it to me and I grabbed it mid air afore it could hit the floor and cause some sorta noise and alert somebody that they was spyin afoot. They was lettering on the shoe and I couldn't make

55

no head nor tell out of o course, but I was sure it was English cause it started with a L and I's pretty sure I had seen that letter afore.

"What's it say Tom?" I asked.

"The beatinist thing," Tom replied, "It says Loafer. Now wonder why anyone would want to brag about being a loafer, even a No Good like Lucifer eye there. Seems to me, even the lazyist among us at least claims to work hard."

"Got me, " I told Tom but I'se agreed with his observation, cause ain't no human ever been lazier than Pap, and he shore claimed to work hard, "And I don't hardly see how it could stay on without no ties."

"Maybe you have to put it on with nails like horses shoes," Tom suggested. "Maybe that's why he ain't wearing im, as It's too painful an affair."

"I'd a damn site go barefoot," I told Tom, which warn't nothing to the telling as I'd a damn site go barefoot instead of wearing tied shoes to unless they's snow out o course,

"Curious," Tom said and let the shoe slip back to the floor. Tom then proceeds to open the suitcase on the floor, and let me just tell you that them shoes that boasted about being a lay about was pure moonshine to what we'ns found next.

They was a shirt on the very top of the pile in the suitcase, and it was the dawgest thing I ever did see. It was dark blue and though it looked like a light cotton fabric, it shore felt more like silk, and it had some funny writing on it. "What's at say?" I asked Tom and showed it to him.

Tom said, "Damn if this guy ain't worsn' we thought," Tom replied,"It says New York Yankees on it. Imagine someone so low down they don't mind admitting they's a Yankee."

That was considerable meanace I allowed then went on with the messing about in the suitcase. They was all sorts of different type clothes in the suitcase. Some being right pretty o course but you wonders about a man that thinks over long on his clothes, and they was for sure, red and blue pants made of a course material that were similar to what I wore which't was cast off cotton pants that had seen better days. But some were just a wonder, and they didn't look like nothing you'd see even at Sunday go to Meeting.

I was almost at the bottom of the pile when I spied the two most curious of things we saw. One was a small ole all over silver thing that I couldn't make no head of at all and the other was a book. Well at least a book was something as Tom could read, but that silver whatzit beat all. I started to mess about with it and something popped up, and you could see it was made fer an eyeball, so I looked into it and I saw Tom and then I figured, this here's a fancy telescope or somen.

Tom just ignored the silver play pretty however and it glommed right on to that book. I never saw Tom look so as he looked when he saw the cover of that book. I can't rightly say that I ever saw anyone look that way, even some fellers that claimed they'd seen ghosts and spooks and whatnot never had that look on they's face.

Tom opened that book and turned a few pages and I o course was looking over his shoulder and they was a picture or two that came into view. They's the dangest pictures too. Now I knows Hannibal Mo ain't the world and that what littlest else I'd seen of the world came from hanging out a balloon or floating down the Missisip, but still, I never seen any buildings like the ones shown. They was even things that looked like they's in the air on one of the pictures, ain't they warn't no hands a holding them up neither.

With a shake of his head Tom said, "Huck this is a book that says what cant be."

Tom always likes to talk in riddles to let on he was more smart than he was, which was powerful enuf, but still everybody likes to put on the dog ever now and agin, but still, the tone he used was more like he meant it than any show putting on.

"How's that Tom?" I asked.

"The title of this book is World History from the 14th – the 21st century," Tom replied.

"Ain't the 21st century a bit further along than we is?" I asked, not being certain as I typically don't know much except that it was Monday or Thursday or Christmas, and didn't think over long on the years that attached to em.

"I'll say," Tom said, "We are in the 19th century. This book contains a history of what ain't happened yet. Which means only one thing."

I naturally thought it meant this here book was a piece of bamboozle that the No Good was gonna try to snake oil some idjit into buying but Tom scotched that notion quick, "This book is from the future," Tom said with more force than he usual talks.

I'se thought it could mean morn that, such as we done lollygagged on this boat a century or two, or else, the book was misprinted by the print setter, them not being the brightest people that ever lived, but then Tom was probably right as he usual was, so I kept my ifs and ands to my self.

"This man must have found a way to travel backards and forwards in time," Tom stated.

"And him a no good Yankee," I replied, "He probably done it out of cussedness."

"Well why ever he done it," Tom continued, "He did do it and that means he was probably the man that shot at Mr. Quatermain. After all, that rifle Mr. Quatermain has looked like wasn't like anything we had ever seen, including him and he's an expert. I bet you that rifle is from the future."

"Maybe it's so Tom," I said, "But I can't rightly figure what's in it for Mr. No Good. After all, if he's really from two or three hundred years on down the road, ain't Mr Quatermain already dead, and if he's already dead, why come back to kill him again?"

"Don't know," Tom said a bit more slowly, "But doubtless he has his reason or maybe he's just a general no good that want's to cause trouble just to be a causing it. Some people are that way."

Now Tom didn't look right at me when he said it, but it hit close to home anyways as some people say that about me. It's mostly true o course, but I denies it when anyone says it cause I like to think of myself as somewhat better a skunk even if it aint' true.

Before Tom could say anythin else, the door suddenly flung open and there stood Mr. No Good himself. I thought, them shoes ain't really loafers, they is skulkers as they shore didn't make no sound afore he showed up and throwed that door open.

I at once started to look about for things to chuck at Mr. No Good, as did Tom, but they wasn't no hard things within common reach, so we just stiffened up and prepared to give our best afore we got knocked about some more, as Mr. No Good, if he was the same man that shot at Mr. Quatermain might be No Good at somethings be he was powerful good with his fists.

"Gentlemen?" Mr No Good said, "To what do I owe this honor?"

The tone of Mr. No Good was plain enough, but his words shore warn't. I think us was doing about anything but being honorable.

Tom didn't say anything to that but instead just went straight to the point. "Mr. are you a Yankee from the future?"

No Good, just smiled at that, "I am not what you think of as a Yankee, as I was born in London England, however, I am from the future."

He said it just like he was saying he was a man, or a Methodist or something else that was just as common as the day is long, which is probably why I belived him. If he had been all dramatic about it, I'd a likely thought he was trying to fool us for some profit.

"Were you the one that tried to kill Mr Quatermain?" Tom continued, "And if you are, prepare to defend yourself."

Tom was more honorable than me, as if No Good had said he was the one what tried to kill Mr. Quatermain, then I'se gonna go at him as skulky as I could, both to do as much damage as quickly as possible, but also cause I'se hoping to catch him by surprise and get thru him and beat feet.

"No," Mr. No Good replied, "I did not try to kill Mr. Quatermain though it is likely we have common enemies."

"How's that, Mr?" Tom enquired.

"Well, whereas I can travel in time, my machine does not travel in space. It stays at the same location for all time. However, during a trip to London a few months ago, I was waylaid by a gang of thieves and somehow they knew where my time ship was located. Whilts I was recovering from the injuries I received in my tussel with them, they made off with the time machine. I ran down one of the thieves in London, mostly because he had too much liquor and had too large a mouth, and I discovered the thieves had taken it to Egypt. I was on their trail, which is how I came to discover they were in Egypt. Now I think, the time ship is still in London, and my trip to Egypt was a diversion."

How a man could talk that long with that many different words was a marvel to behold, but No Good did just that.

"You shore you didn't just fergit where you put it?" I asked as I often accused Pap of stealing stuff and he often did, but sometimes he didn't and I liked to cover all possibilities.

"I'm pretty sure I didn't, Master," then he stopped for a minute and said, "What exactly are your names anyway?"

"I'm Tom and this is Huck," Tom replied, then continued "How'd you get a time ship, Mr. ..." and Tom let his sentence end in an uptake so No Good would know we wanted a name to attached to him.

"You may call me Mr. Smith. As to the time machine, I must admit, I inherited it, though it was as much an accident as it was on purpose. My ancestor invented the ship and after some adventures, locked it in a shed with a warning that the use of the machine could wreck the space time continuum. When I found it by accident and being a renegade at heart I ignored the warning, much to my regret and possibly's to mankind's regret," and I knowed right away, even after the short time that I knew Mr.

Smith, that there wouldn't be any short discussions as long as he's a part of em.

"So you think these thieves have not only stolen your time ship, but they are also using it to change history?" Tom asked. He was a wonder, as he saw right off that anyone that could flit about in time could pretty much change anything they's wanted to suit themselves but then again Tom had been thinking about time already and he weren't hampered by being a Pentecostal so as me. Course he may be going to hell cause he weren't no Pentecostal, but that's another thing altogether.

"Yes, I think there are a group of bad men that have found my ship. Luckily, I have rendered it immobile from traveling in time, but they likely will solve that problem eventually. I must get it back before that, and get back to my own time, or at least destroy the ship before it is used for some deviltry," Mr. Smith stated.

"What be this Mr. Smith," I asked, and showed him the silver doodad I was holding.

"That is a camera Huck," Mr. Smith answered as if that was an answer.

"What be a camera?" Tom and I asked almost together but enough together that Tom said "Bread and Butter," to hold off the bad luck that entailed.

Mr. Smith said, "It takes pictures, let me show you."

Mr. Smith took the camera thingee, and punched and prodded and soon said, "Look in this eyepiece

Huck."

Well look I did, but I was a bit cautious about it, cause just cause a man says he ain't bad don't mean he ain't bad and who knew what could happened when I looked at somein I knew nothing about, but still look I did.

I put my eye to where Mr. Smith pointed and lo and behold, it was Tom Sawyer and myself lookin back at me. "Tom," I cried, "This ain't possible, but you and I is in this ere thing the same as we is ere."

That sentence made no sense to Tom a first, but as quick as he came over and looked at it with me he understood.

"Never heard of a picture that warn't drawn," I said. "Is this some kinda devil work?"

"Just science Huck." Mr Smith answered. "Some might say that science is the Devil's work, but it is probably no more so than any other human activity."

"Do you think the gun that was used to shoot at Mr. Quatermain was from the future?" asked Tom.

"Possibly," Mr. Smith answered, "Describe it."

Tom described how it was all silver and didn't use no bullets and was made by some firm that Mr Quatermain had never heard of and didn't think exist.

"That is from the future," Mr. Smith said, "As it is my gun. Undoubtedly the assassin had determined how to use the rifle, possibly to the detriment of mankind. I do believe that at least one of the thieves that stole my ship is somewhere on this ship, as I know he traveled to Egypt. Doubtless he is using a different name now."

"Could you identify this rifle if we brought it to you Mr. Smith?" Tom asked.

"With certitude," Mr. Smith answered, which I took it to mean yes but didn't really know, and we all know people like Mr. Smith that always chooses the uncommon word as if to show he was so much smarter than you.

"Well, you just wait here Mr. Smith," Tom said, "And we'll go bring Mr. Quatermain back with the rifle."

"That would be most appreciated," Mr. Smith stated, and then stood aside from the front of the door to let us out, and out we went, tho I think I was just a little bit in more of a hurry than Tom so I scooted out first. Tom walked out more leisurely as they say, but then again Tom was more trusting than I, wich was probly a good thing, but then Tom hadn't grew up with Pap, so there might be just some justification for my lack of trust.

6

Quartermain's Sleep is Disturbed

There are rooms on this boat and then there are rooms. Me and Huck was sharing a room, o' course, and it warn't the most roomy room you could think of, but it was enuf for me and Tom ad we only slept there anyway as it is uncommon hard to do much spyin from inside your bedroom. Mr. Quatermain on the other hand had a bunch a rooms, with an inner and outer, much as a house has, and they even called the outer room a parlour, thou I think it was somewhat odd to call it that as it didn't have no pianer as all of them do in Hannibal.

As we came to the parlour we saw that a bunch of Mr. Quatermain's hired hands was a playing poker and it weren't for funnsies either like when men

Tom play as they was a wad a cash on the table.

Now I'se got to enterduce some of them others besides Otumpo that works for Mr. Quatermain, mostly cause the story father along is gonaa depend on you knowing these men. They was one guy called Lyndon, who was a white man that spoke like a Scotsman, but he was browner than even I was, which meant he spent some time in the sun for sure. There was some Ayerab called Ali which seemed to be one of the only names they's allowed in Ayerab as I never met a man there that weren't called either Muhhamed or Ali. Then there was a Chinese man pretending to be a Japanese named Haruto.

In order to kinda be natural like, we didn't try to run by Utumbo, also cause he was a lot bigger'n us and might try to stop our entry so we stood to the back of the table and pretended to watch the poker game.

Haruto won a hand and smiled as he raked in the winnings and he said to Utumbo, "It's lucky Mr. Quatermain pays you so well as you will need it after this night."

Utumbo just laughed with the rest of em and said, "I'll want for nothing after this night, if we let honest men deal for a change," but he laughed when he said it, so Haruto didn't sock him tho even if he hadda laughed he'd gotten bopped but good in Hannibal for saying that.

The poker game was interestin enough I guess but Tom and me had other and more important fish to fry and we aimed to just kinda slip on by this group and go into see Mr. Quatermain, but Utumbo just looked up when we tried to skulk by and said, "Tom and Huck, stop that," and I was fortunate enuf to be fer enuf away from his reach to save myself a bop on the head. "Mr Quatermain asleep and want to stay that way. You come back tomorrow."

This was noways in our plans of course, as we needed to get Mr. Quatermain in touch with Mr. Smith sooner rather than later to set history right, or prevent history from being changed, or to see if we us predestined or what not or somethin. Tom of course wouldn't let Otumbo stop hem, as he wouldn't let anyone stop him when he got a head o steam up, so out comes Tom's most dangerous weapon which was his mouth.

"They's a lady on deck that has done lost her skirt and petticoat," Tom said, "And I just thought Mr. Quatermain might want to be chilvarous and help that lady."

"Tom why you not spoke earlier," Utumbo said and he and each of the poker players got religion all of a sudden as they quit playing cards and headed for the door.

Tom was leading the pack on the way out, so that he could dodgem about the boat and give me time to get to Mr. Quatermain. Of course, I headed right for Mr. Quatermain's bedroom as quick as I saw the back of the last man as they went out.

I opened the door and heard Mr. Quatermain

cutting logs as we all do when we's asleep. I walked over to his bed to grab his shoulder and wake him up gentle like and just as I was about to touch him, I is ashamed to say, I almost shrieked like a girl and I ain't ashamed to say I jumped back. Right there, just next to Mr. Quatermain on the bed was a scorpion with the awfulest disposition as anyone was likely to see.

The scorpion was wandering to and fro about the bedspread and moving his tail as he did. Now I knowed that the scorpion is natural enuf a meanun that he would sooner rather than later put that tail into Mr. Quatermain, so I did what anybody else'd do and I grabbed a book off the table besides the bed and bopped that scorpion. Trouble is, I missed the scorpion and bopped Mr. Quatermain instead.

Alan Quatermain came a tumbling out of his bed and the covers went ever which way and that scorpion went up in the air and tail out straight headed for me. I jumped as fast and as far as I could to the left hoping the scorpion was gonna head right, and the Lord musta benn with me cause that's what happened. Quatermain screamed, "Why you rascal, I was trying to slumber,"

I shouted, "You just about slumbered your way to purgatory," and I pointed at the scorpion on the floor, that was scattering as fast as its legs were possible towards the bed again.

I thought that Quatermain had leaped fair when I had hit him with a book, but that leap was second class compared to what he did when he saw that scorpion. Mr. Quatermain, went up and out and practically over as he put distance between himself and that scorpion.

"Beware Huck," Quatermain shouted, "That's a dangerous scorpion," which was nice o him to say o course, but I had alredy come to that conclusion or I wouln't tried to bop it to start with, being a natural-ist as much as possible and having let even ratllers go when I saw no good reason to killem.

Mr. Quatermain grabbed the book I had tried to commit mayhem with and finished the work, but fair. He hit that poor scorpion every which way from Sunday and what was left was a smudge no biggern a grease stain from Ms Purdy's cooking, then he gets a newspaper and put the remainder of that scorpion onto it, then threw it out the little winder he had in his room.

"Thank you Huck," Mr Quatermain said, "You have doubtless saved my life," which was true, but I had saved my own life to and I was more proud of that, regardless of how well I thought of Mr. Qua-termain.

"How did you know to come in and save me, Huck?" Mr Quatermain wanted to know.

"Cause, I found a time traverler that wants to speak with you and he thinks he can explain that gun that pot shotted at you and would like to see it and I still ain't made up my mind on any pre-destination," I said in plain Hannibal English, but

Mr. Quatermain acted like he couldn't understand. Well you's got to make allowances fer the ignorant I reckon and all of us are ignorant about something.

Bout the time I got through speaking as clear as possible to Mr. Quatermain, Tom comes in and says "The lady without skirt and without petticoat ain't there no longer," with a huge smile on his face.

Quatermain begins to shake his head and he mumbled something like (Lord help me) thou he might've said (Lord help them), either way I thought it was a good sentiment.

"Tom," Quatermain said sharply, "I need facts and need them now. Why are you and Huck in my bedroom, even though I am thankful that Huck saved my life."

Now Tom was the one that was looking a quizzed on his face. "How'd Huck save your life Mr. Quatermain?"

"Why didn't you send him in to kill that scorpion that almost got me?" Quatermain asked.

"Not no how did I send him in to do anything except to get the gun that you took from the man in the burka," Tom said, "As we think we know who that gun was stolen from and wanted to get you to take it to him to discuss things."

"That is news," Quatermain exclaimed, "And something I greatly wish to discuss. Let me get the gun and we will proceed to meet this Gentleman, who is?"

"Mr Smith," Tom said, "That is, if you believe

him, and I do about the gun but not about the name, though why he would lie about it is beyond me."

Quatermain, if he had a reply to that, didn't reply, instead he just smiled and then walked over to a chest of drawers that was just under the little winder. He pulled out a drawer and then he froze, and turned slowly and looked at us. "The rifle is gone!!"

7

The Meeting of
Quartermain & Smith

"**I** ain't took it," I said out of force of habit, and Mr. Quatermain didn't even look at me so I guess I warn't in his sights as a thief to start with, which was good but highly unusual cause anytime I'se someplace in Hannibal and something is missing people look rights at me, and typically with good reason.

Mr Quatermain didn't say anything for a few seconds, just stood there and kinda thought about things, or at least pretended to think about things, which is what I typically do when I aint' got nothing better to do. Then he said, "I must meet this man who says the rifle is his. Maybe he has already reclaimed his property," which was polite words for stole it back.

Tom lead the way out of the bedroom and into the

parlour. None of the poker players had returned yet, them havin their exercise rushing about the building lookin for that woman that had lost her clothes. I reckoned Tom had led them a merry chase then ditchted them, which I'se knows from experience he is mighty accomplished at.

"Where is Utumbo?" Quatermain said but it warn't particularly to anyone.

"I am at fault for Utumbo not being here," Tom admitted, then told Mr. Quatermain how he had made up that tale about the lady cavorting about without no clothes on. "I had to tell a little white lie to give Huck a chance to see you." That's Tom for you, he was modest to a fault as anyone that would call that whopper a little white lie was the modestest person in the world.

A great big smile came over Mr. Quatermain's face and he said, "Tom you are a genius of the first rank. Right up there with Sir Issac Newton."

A great big smile came over Tom when he heard this, but I warn't to sure it was much of a compliment. Everybody had heard of Issac Newton o course, even an uneducated person like me. He was the man that was too stupid to get outta the way of a falling apple, and when it hit him on the head he said, Gravity what done it. It don't take no genius to know that an apple falls down, as they always do, so I never did understand why people thought he was so smart. If he had a seen an apple fall down, then stop mid fall do the hootchie-kootchie and turn a flip then fly off into the sky for parts unknown, then says, that's gravity, well then I coulda thought he was a genius. But Tom seemed to accept the compliment as it was given, and not as one of those he does the best he can compliments, which is what I typically gets.

Mr. Smith was awaiting with bate breath as they say, which means he was anxious to see Mr. Quatermain about that there rifle, and when we came in and I commenced to tell him about the naked woman that didn't exist and the scorpion that did exist and that Mr. Quatermain had done losted the gun but I ain't took it, he smiled and then says to Mr. Quatermain, "I am to be called Mr. Smith," and he extended his hand, "And you I take it are Allan Quatermain the famous explorer."

"Must I admit it," Mr. Quatermain said and laughed, though I thought he might be afraid this guy was really some lawman after him about something and didn't want to own up to who he was just in case.

The two men commenced to palavering and me and Tom just kinda listened in. I can't guarantee I understood every word as the English they spoke, ifen it was English, were a might different than the English I spoke. Not everyone howsever is fortunate enuf to be from Hannibal MO so I made allowances.

"Tom and Huck have told me that you have a silver rifle that shoots air not bullets but is just as deadly even so," Mr. Smith said to Mr. Quatermain. "I have good reason to believe that the rifle is mine."

"Had, is the proper word, as it is missing from my chest of drawers where I had placed it," Mr. Quter-main replied. "It was replaced with a nasty little scorpion which may have had the better of me had Huck not so fortuitously visted."

"It seems," Mr Smith replied, "That there is a common conspiracy against us, and I must say, they are using my weapons to their betterment. I don't know why you were targeted however."

"Nor do I," admitted Mr. Quatermain, "But I am more interested in whether you came from the future as the boys would have it. I must say that beggars the imagination."

"An understatement," Mr. Smith replied with a trace of a smile on his lips. "It is true however, as my great, great, great, great whatzit invented a time machine. He caused enough trouble in the future that he eventually returned the time ship to London England and stored it with proper warning not to use it. Myself not being always of right mind, ignored his warning and come to my current pre-dictament. Somehow the ruffians that have been after you, also stole my machine and stranded me here in the 1840s."

"Then you would have it sir, and not in jest of course," Quatermain stated quite without a trace of humor in his voice, "That you are indeed from the future."

"I would good sir," Mr. Smith replied, and then he commenced to showing Mr. Quatermain some of the things that Huck and I had found in his suitcase. Even Mr. Quatermain who had likely done and seen a site more things than Tom and I put together, was awusmated by what he saw.

"This is truly a history of the future?" Mr. Quatermain asked as he looked over the book Mr. Smith had handed.

"Your future, my past, rather confusing what," Mr Smith understated as it was powerful confusin to me.

"To say the least," Quatermain replied.

"I do believe that there is more than one person involved in the theft of my vehicle," Mr. Smith continued, "Likely much more than one, as the time ship was rather heavy and difficult to be moved by just one person. Also, I had left things with the vehicle such as the rifle that was used to attack you and clothing and other books that could be put to use in a bad way by those that are of a wont to do so. Since the vehicle was last in London, I assume it is still there and that I was lured to Egypt just to get me out of the way for awhile."

"Meaning?" Quatermain asked.

"If you knew there would be a war at a certain place and at a certain time between certain nations, couldn't you stand to profit," Mr. Smith said, tho it made no sense to me as the only ones I would think would profit from war would be undertakers.

"Or possibly," Mr. Smith continued, "If you did not like the outcome written in the book, you could attempt to change it. I am here to tell you that it may be a possibility that the future, is not fixed, as the past contains the seeds of the future, and anyone that knows anything about horticulture knows that the seeds will only grow if planted."

"We must then," Mr. Qutermain stated, "Find the attempted murderer and all others that would attempt to profit from ill gotten gain. I am tempted," Mr. Quateramin continued, "To determine what lies ahead for my nation in this book and I am also ashamed of the thought that I would do so. The future is in God's hands and is not meant for man to interfere with it's rightful course. No insult meant, Mr. Smith, but you really should not have opened this particular Pandora's box."

"I acknowledge the admonishment," replied Mr. Smith, "But there is a saying that is still valid in both your time and mine, there is no use crying over spilled milk. Since what is done, is in fact done, we now must make sure that we do our best to minimize the damage that will result from this particular problem."

"A man should always learn from his mistakes, and I take it, you wish to find your time ship and determine what this conspiracy's purpose is in taking the ship from you," Mr. Quatermain said.

"That is so," answered Mr. Smith, "And since the rifle that tried to take your life is mine, I wish to retrieve it and all the other things from the future to ensure that they do not cause damage to this time line. I also think, that someone in your party must be part of this conspiracy, else the rifle would not have gone missing."

"Well I don't know that I follow that logic," Mr. Quatermain admitted, "As there are other people aboard this vessel."

"True that," Mr. Smith replied, "However, those other people are unlikely to be involved as I have played detective and had conversations with them. Most are of old British stock and that would be an unlikely disguise as it would be too easy to unravel the truth."

I could see on Mr. Quatermain's face that he wasn't overly fond of that argument, but then, as he admitted, "You may be right as most of my people are in fact, of little money or title and are as likely to be able to manufacture an identity as they are to have a true identity, but I would like to think I was a better judge of character than to hire a snake for my doings, though it must be admitted, I wouldn't want a saint for the work I am involved in. Still someone on this ship must be involved or else they would not have known to search for the rifle."

They went on like that for quite a spell talking in riddles, and such. But the basic points was they would work together to uncover this conspiracy and to get aholdt of the time ship and other things from the future. Then Mr. Smith would go back to whince he came and the time space whatacal-lit wouldn't be subverted by them's that would do meanace. Let's I think that's what they said. Mr Quatermain wound it up by saying, "I will talk to my men to determine if any have the possibility of being the culprit," which was finery speak for say-ing, I'll find the skunk if he exists.

Tom was listening more to this palavering than was I and he said, "I will also try to think of a way to find the culprit." The men didn't pay him no never mind, o course as old folks don't generally like to hear nothing form young uns but yes sir and no maam, but I have grown to respect's Tom's thinking ability moren most and I figured, Tom would do just that.

8

Finding the Culprit

The next day the ship was ready to land at London and you never seen such a sight in your life. Men was busy running hither and thither, lifting this and shouting words you don't hear in church in the process. It was one of the few times that boat could light a candle agin a paddle wheeler of the Missisip.

Tom's thinking had lead him to putting on some outrageous outfit that he had taken from Mr. Smith's suitcase. He was wearing a pink shirt that seemed to glow, and some of them purple pants that looked like cotton but werent' and a hat that had some sorta ball on it and letters I didn't understand and all of it was a way too big for him. He was as gaudy as any gal I had ever seen in her ball gown, but being a nice person I didn't tell Tom as I didn't think he would take it as a compliment. Tom was a strutting like a peacock and was otherwise making a spectical of hisself, which was the plan as I was watching to see who was paying any attention to him.

While Tom was up to his shenanigans and I was seeing if anyone paid any attention to him or else just ignored him like he was a simpleton, Mr. Quatermain was having a meeting with his men. Fortunate like, I could see in the winder where he was talking to them or rather shouting at em as tha't what it seemed, and still kinda look over the people to see if any was paying any never mind to Tom. I have taken out some of Mr. Quatermain's language below, as the church going might be a reading this.

" You men," Mr.Quatermain said (and unnecessary to as they weren't a woman among um), "Likely know that the rifle I recovered in my tussle with the assassin in Egypt is missing. Since only you men knew of the existence it stands to reason that one of you may have had a hand in the removal of the rifle from my drawer. It pains me to think that anyone in my employ would turn traitor to me, but that's the most likely answer. Does anyone have anything to say?"

None of em said nuttin of course, as he who speaks might draw attention and when the boss is busy chewing, the last thing you want from him is attention.

"Very well," Mr Quatermain said, "Then I have the unpleasant duty of searching each of you and searching your premises," premises being where they's sleep at night o course, tho they might not of known it. "If there are any objections, I need to hear them now."

Mr. Quatermain was looking just at Utumbo just when he was saying these things and I admits I felt sorry for him, as he was sweating and I don't think it was just cause the heat.

My attention was drawn back to Tom as he continued about his carrying on. He was shouting and making a general nuisance of hisself by screaming stuff like "I know the future, I know the future, the Ottoman empire is doomed, man will go to the moon, I know the future."

Well them that was paying some attention to him before shore weren't now. It's one thing to think a man is acting silly but it's another to think him insane and that were what Tom seemed to be. I'se o course just looked trying to see if anyone was looking and not just laughing but so far the only thing I saw was a few dock hands laughing and pointing and a few ladies doing their best to not look, thou they was laughing a bit whilst they didn't look.

I heard Quatermain's voice rise agin, so I natural like shifted my gaze back through the winder. "The people you serve," Mr. Quatermain said, and agin I thought he was directing his eyes toward Utumbo, "Are evil. They are trying to change the future, may even be from the future, but whomever or whatever they are, they have no allegiance to you or to this time. They have reckoned only that they may profit from knowledge they have and that others do not. You may profit yourself, at least temporarily but if these people change history, it may mean that you have placed yourself at their mercy without even realizing it."

Them was so long words for the men Mr. Quatermain had hired, but sure, as they hadn't gone to Eaton or Harvard or even to good ole Thomas Jefferson elementary in Hannibal Mo, but to look at they's faces you'd know they understood.

Mr. Quatermain then did the dangest thing, he walked right up to Otumpo, put his face not moren and inch from him and said, "If any of you know anything, you had best tell me or else face even worse consequences," although what could be worse than a mad Mr. Quatermain was beyond me.

Suddenly they came Mr. Smith to the door of the meeting room and looked in, he gave a secret sign to Mr. Quatermain which was the thumbs up, and only thems that had a second grade education would understand it meant something. Well as I allow that the men that worked for Mr. Quatermain warn't college men, they was at least some educated as they knew right away something was up.

"Mr Smith," Mr. Quateramin continued, with his eyes intently on Utumbo's face, "Has just finished checking each of your rooms and he did not find the gun. That means either you have gotten away with passing the rifle to your co-conspirator, or else you have it hidden somewhere else. Mr. Smith, of course, will continue his search as we quietly stare at each other, and if he finds it, then we will have plenty to discuss."

As Mr. Smith started to open up some of the cabinet drawers that were siterated about the room, I noticed some sudden movement. Someone jumped at the table and suddenly I saw the silver rifle come out in his hands. Afore anything else could happen, I saw a knife whistle, straighter than any arrow was ever shot and it plunged into the man that had the silver gun's shoulder, knocking him back and causing him to stumble.

Mr. Smith leaps on the man as quick as Panthee and starts a rasseling with the man and the next thing you knows, Mr. Smith has the rifle and is looking down at the man, which was the Chinese Haruto, grabbing aholdt of him and pulling him to his feet. "I have you my good friend," Mr. Smith said, thou I thought he was stretchin it abit calling the no good that was aiming to pot shot Mr. Quartermain a friend.

Mr. Haruto said, "American Dogs will never defeat the Rising Sun!" then he just went limp in Mr. Smith's arms and naturally collapsed to the floor. What in hell he meant by his words I didn't know and I could tell Mr. Quatermain was a bit puzzled to, I mean, I didn't know any dogs, much less, dogs in America had any sort a tussle with the Sun. Few of em didn't like the moon o course but I didn't think their howlin at it upset the moon any.

With the man on the floor, and I knows he had a knife in his shoulder but that didn't look like it would make a grown man pass out, but it had, Mr. Quatermain came over and leaned down to look at him, and make sure he warn't playing possum. Mr. Quatermain shook him, then said, "What's that odor?"

"Burnt Almonds," Mr. Smith said, which made no sense as Haruto hadn't been eating anything much less almonds and who'd want to eat burnt ones anyway?

"Which means something to you?" Mr. Quatermain said to Mr. Smith.

"Yes," replied Mr. Smith, "He has killed himself by taking a poison called cyanide."

"And the last words?" asked Quatermain.

"History will show why those words are important and they may go part way to explaining the conspiracy, though it doesn't explain why you are so important they wish to kill you," Mr Smith explained, sorta kinda.

Mr. Quatermain just shrugged his shoulders and said, "I will take you at your word, as you have superior knowledge to me on this issue," then he stood up from the floor and winked at Utumbo. "Thank you good friend for being my protector as well as allowing me to use you to force the real criminal to reveal himself."

Utumbo just walked over and pulled the knife out of Mr. Haruto, then he smiled and said, "Knife quicker than gun sometimes," and he put the knife back into the holder at his side.

"In your hands," Quatermain said, "The knife is quicker than the gun all the time."

Mr. Smith was examining the rifle that he had snatched from Haruto and was examining it and said, "This is my rifle, though why this Japanese man wanted to kill you with it, still evades me. "

"Me to," Quatermain responded, "I hired Mr Haruto in Egypt, and he was a reliable man for what little hunting I did with him. I suppose he could have killed me a dozen times over but didn't, and that is another mystery as to why he waited, and after waiting why make a reckless move for the rifle here, after all, if we found it in a common area, I doubt we would have thought him the culprit any more than any one else."

"I don't think it was his job to kill you, but to keep an eye on you and let others know of your location. He panicked and tried to get the rifle, I believe, because he had been entrusted with retrieving it and passing it back to some other that is part of the conspiracy. Just a conjecture of course," but Bob's your Uncle, if it isn't proven out."

I didn't know that Mr. Quartermain had an Uncle o course and was real surprised that Mr. Smith knew it, but then again he was from the future and likely knows more than I do about these things.

9

On the Dock

While all them doings was agoing on in the meeting room on the boat, Tom was astill a makin a spectacle of hisself, shouting about moon rocks, and wars to come, and a bowl a (he pronounced it e bowl a but I figures he meant a bowl a) something that was gonna kill all us hetherns. I reminded myself that the sideshow was over and my job was to see if I could see someone that was doing more than just makin fun of Tom.

Then I sees him, and it was the man that had tried to pot shot Mr. Quatermain al right as his eyes was the eviliest and he had a busted nose from my right hook, and it gives me more pleasure than the Lord would think right, to say that. That man was a staring and a staring and a frowning and a frowning and maybe it was his disposition but I was sure he didn't like what he was a hearin and seeing.

"Tom!," I shouts, "There be the no good assassin," and pointed at him on the dock. Well that man did not wait around for no invitation but started to beat feet as fast as he could away from us.

Me'n Tom ain't the strongest people in the world but we is spry on our feet and we jumped ofen the boat and headed towards where that man had been. We didn't knock down morn' two or three people in the process.

"Come back here you no good assassin," Tom hollers out and yells even louder, "Somebody stop that man."

After we had bounced off two or three other people, mostly cause they's in the way and were to onery to get outta the way, we had almost lost site of the assassin when a man in a blue suit wearing a funny hat steps into our path and says "Whoa you rapscallions,".

Well we showed him what rapscallions could really do as Tom hits him high and I hits him load and he fell down. As he fell down, he pulled out a whistle and started blowing it to beat the band. Tom yells, "That's a London Bobby," which set me to wondering if Tom knowed people I didn't and whether he was Mr. Quatermain's uncle who was also named Bob, but I had no more time to ponder as we saw the assassin bounce off a feller himself and the guy seemed irritated as he gave him a big push. The assassin went right into the river which is called Tim's but is spelt Thames, which shows you that furriners can't always spell any better than Americans.

Mr. Assassin had just started to wail, "I can't swim," when Tom and me comes up and Tom grabs a holdt of a rope and says, "I'm going in after him, hold the rope so he don't panic and take me under," and Tom jumped with one end a the rope in his hand and I took the other end and wrapped it around a big ole dock outing and holdt it for good measure.

Tom proceeds to the assassin, and then the assassin's screams out some word I didn't understand and grabs aholdt of Tom and they both disappears beneath the river. I don't mind admitting, I thought Tom was a gonner as well as the assassin, but then I feels a tug on the rope and I starts to reel it in like a fishin line.

There came the assassin up, lookin a lot worse than he had goin in, and Tom naturally just comes up a few feet away with that grin on his face I knows so well. He had slipped that rope around the assassin, then had gone deeper likely, as drownin folks will let go a you if you goes deeper but'll hold on for dear life if you tires to go up. Tom had been on a many a swimmin journey with me and he knowd that from experience, as did I but I doubt I'd been cool enough to go deeper when someone had aholdt of me, but woulda likely panicked myself and got both of us drowned.

Just as I was a pulling the assassin out, Mr. Quateramin, Utumbo and Mr Smith comes a running up, they had seen me at the end o the pier and had thought I needed help, which I did considerable need and was glad to gets. Between us, we had easy pickings pulling the assassin outa the water and up to the shore. Just as soon as he came up, Mr Smith, steps up to him and belts him one, then he reaches into his mouth and pulls out a tooth. "We don't want to lose this man as we did the other," Mr Smith said, just as Tom rejoined the team. Now Tom hadn't seen what was goin on in the meeting room so he just kinda looked quizzical at Mr. Smith, so I puts in my 2 cents worth, "The Chinese guy kilt hisself after he tried to kill Mr Quatermain, but Utumbo got him in the shoulder with his knive then when they got the rifle back the guy eat burnt almonds which he musta been highly allergic to as he died rite on the spot," which was about as plain as it could be told but Tom's face didn't brighten as he got the knowledge.

"I'll tell you later Tom," Mr. Quatermain stated, "But it is with great relief I do say that we have obtained the futuristic rifle that was used to make an attempt on my life, and we do have the gentleman in custody, thanks to you and Huck, and the Chinese person Mr. Huck alluded to was actually a Japanese man named Haurto."

I'se could tell from his face that Tom was some relieved that the rifle had been gotten back and he was a course pleased we captured the assassin, but he was like me, and thought that Mr. Quatermain shoulda knowed a Chinese man when he seed one, but he kept his silence on the issue.

Abouts this time the assassin gets over his frights and said, "Death before dishonor," which is a noblest sentiment but didn't hardly make no sense since no one was afixin to kill him, then he did something with his mouth that looked like he was cracking a hickory nut. His eyes flinched fer a minute then they got as wide as a raccoon's. "What.." he said, and then he sees that Mr. Smith was aholding his tooth, which made him let fly with some words that weren't honorable at least most preachers don't think they's honorable.

"We will have a discussion on many is- sues," Mr. Smith says to the assassin, "Not the least of which will be where is my time ship." "You will get nothing but static from me," the assas- sin said, which was strange cause I knows Im uned- ucated but you can often tell what something meant from the way it's said, even if you don't' know the words, but I didn't know what static meant and if it meant nothing why not say nothing but then, I am uneducated as I said, and o course Mr. Smith caught on right away.

"We will see," Mr. Smith said, and it warn't like any words I ever heard from him afore, as they were as full of fright as a man could make em, "We will see."

10

At the Zoo

Mr. Quartermain had lead us all to the
London Zoo. He told me and Tom that he had
plenty of friends at the Zoo as he had given' em an-
imal or two every now and again and they would
leave us talk to the assassin at our own pace and not
disturb us. Having friends is useful no doubt but I
did notice him slipping some paper money to the
guy that let us in, but that was pure courtesy I guess,
and no how's influenced the guy who'd a let us in
just cause he was a friend of Mr. Quatermain but
every body had to earn a living.

The London zoo was a strange place for a boy
from Hannibal, Mo and likely for a boy from anywhere. They was animals there I'd never seed afore
and they was some that was as cute as could be
and some that warn't so cute but probly weren't no

meaner a rattler, who ain't really none mean anyways as he'll leave you alone if you'll leave him alone, but I've heard tell that cotton mouths are just mean and won't just leave you alone but then you hears all sortsa things.

There was a cage that held somen that was somewhere altogether odder than anything in Hannibal Mo, and that was somen called a goriller. This goriller, weren't no man they said, but was a homi somn or other but he was just plan ugly to me and natural enuf, he started to beat his chest and spit and growl and make all sorts a noise as we came inside the room where he was caged. This was handy as Mr. Quatermain had done put that assassin right up to the cage that held that goriller. To say that the assassin warn't to happy about it, woulda been to tell a bunch o truth.

"Get me away from this beast," the assassin screamed, and struggled to get out of the hands of Mr. Quatermain and Utumbo and Mr. Smith, but squirming and shouting didn't do no good as they was three men and they was strong.

"Where is my Time Ship?" demanded Mr. Smith. "Why do you want to kill Mr. Quartermain?" he shouted. "Who do you work with?"

"Get me away from this beast," the assassin screamed again, "I'll talk," which no one believed he would do if he was takin away from the beast but he talked right enuf, casue the beast managed to put a hand through the cage and get aholdt of his hair.

One swift jerk and he screamed, "I"ll talk, I'll talk," and he did good and plenty.

Mr. Quatermain and Mr. Smith pulled the man away from that goriller and I've never seen a man any happier, and that includes Pap when he has just stolen a jug of corn liqquer. They pulled the assassin to a chair in the middle of the room, close enuf to the goriller to have it remind the man of why he's talking but fer enuf away to hear what he said.

"I don't know why Quatermain is on the kill list," the assassin said, and he was as calm as a man that had almost been et by a goriller could be, "But he is, as are you, calling your self Smith as I understand it, and others throughout the centuries. Best be on your guard," and a small smile passed his lips, which didn't make no sense but he did it anyways.

"Why would you want to kill me and why would you want to kill Smith and any others?" Quatermain demanded to know. "I've done nothing to you, have I?"

"Admittedly you have not," the Assassin replied, "But I work for a much higher power, and one that has the advantages that Mr. Smith has. They can travel through time and they know that you must be destroyed, and they have good reason, and so must Mr. Smith and Mr. Smith must not be allowed to travel to other times, as his ancestor did, because, every cause has an effect and every effect is amplified throughout time. Mr. Smith's bungling has already caused many problems for the world, and will continue to cause problems unless he is eliminated and we eliminate his effects on the timeline."

The assassin said all o this with a straight face and I gotta tell you it was considerable hard to believe. Even if you can travel in time and change things, then how come somebody that travels backs and unchanges them, don't himself cause other changes, and then would somebody else come along and un-changed what you had unchanged so it was changed again. This weren't nothing but a bunch of head-aches, when it cames to the logic department.

Mr. Quatermain was standing behind the assas-sin now and I saw him jerk his head to one side. Utumbo gave a quick nod and then left the room, as silent as a snake slithering through the grass. I didn't pay it no never mind, as kids don't usual pay adults no never mind, but it would have a meaning o course and not a small reason either.

"Then you claim to be a fellow time traveler?" Mr Smith asked the assassin.

"I claim, nothing," the assassin answered, "I am a time traveler and a member of the Brotherhood. Our aim is to restore history to it's rightful path. I was born in 1955, if that matters. When one can travel in time a year has no meaning at all, only events have meanings."

"Possibly," Mr. Smith said, "But one is always influenced by how he was raised, and can't always refute the reigns placed on him by the sentiments which raised him and that is often influenced more by the times during which he was raised as much as by any religious conviction or other family influence." Which was fancy talk for, you can take the boy outta the country but you can't take the country outta the boy.

"There is truth in many platitudes," the assassin responded, "But there is not total truth in them. I was recruited by a group of right thinking men, men that understand that human destiny must be shaped, to ensure that earth will one day become a paradise and not the hell hole it has been for mankind throughout history. We call ourselves the Brotherhood, because it is both a statement on our mission and it is how we view ourselves."

"Your group," Smith continued, "Believes that they of course, know what's best for mankind, and of course that has been the fatal conceit of every totalitarian that has ever existed."

"When one can experiment in time and see the results in history, it is more than a conceit," the assassin said. "If we do not see our desires come to fruition in the future, then we know we must have another change, and the beauty of it is that we can see our results immediately as we have people at both ends of the time line, with one doing the changing and another the observing. It is no longer a conceit, Mr. Smith, it is history."

Me and Tom was listening to all of this going's back and forth and while I suspect Tom understood most of it, the cabbage warn't chawed fine enough for me to swaller it, but I did my best. I also's began to wonder why Mr. Quatermain was staying as quite as a mouse and why Utumbo had walked away, quite like. But then I wonders a lot about things and I ain't ashamed to admit I don't always gets answers to my wonders.

"Where is my time ship," Mr. Smith asked again. "If you can travel in time, then you hardly need mine, so please give it to me, then we can both play what games we will play as we travel hither and yon through the pages of history. We can even wave at each other as one undoes the others' error," which was one of them unfunny jokes that adults tells and smiles slightly at, but it wouldn't get anything but rude noises from mosta the boys I knows if they heard it.

"Your time ship, is being well taken care of," the assassin replied, with just a shade of a smile crossing his lips. "you of course, will never see it again."

Suddenly the door opened as did a couple of winders and there were men in black uniforms, holding them silver rifles and aiming them at everyone in the room, including me, which I didn't care fore no how. I could see the surprise come to Mr. Smith as his eyes flew open, then I looked at Mr. Quatermain and all I saw was them same blue eyes you always see and a face without expression. Him being a hunter, I thought would mean they warn't much to fool you as animals are a lot smarter than most people knows and he'd probably been outfoxed moren' once or twice, and maybe even out-foxed by a fox.

"I do believe gentlemen and young lads," the as-sassin said as smooth as the Missisip when the wind warn't blowing, "That the shoe is now on the other foot," which was fancy for, gots you with yore pants down I did.

Mr. Quatermain spoke for the first time in quite some while, "I ask for nothing for myself, nor for Mr. Smith, as we are grown men who were foolish enough not put out a sentry, and me an experienced hunter, but I do ask that you allow the boys to go free. Tom and Huck can do you no harm, for even if they talked it would be dismissed as the fantasy's of a child."

"On that you may be correct," the assassin said, "But even so, me must test whether their demise at this time will impact history, and the only way we can do that is to kill them. If we choose to, of course, we can come back and prevent them from ever meeting up with you in the first place, but that has yet to be determined as an appropriate action. They may well wind up alive, but enough of this banter, we must make haste before your Umptombo returns with whomever you dispatched him for."

Then I seeds what Mr. Quatermain had tried to do, he had tried to put Umptombo out to prevent the no goods help from coming to his aid and to let us know when trouble was abrewing, but evident-ly somethin had gone amiss, as they says as the no goods had got to us anyhows's. While I thought that, another thought came to me, if they can prevent us from dying by preventing us from meeting Quatermain, why hadn't they already done so, after all, the assassin was bragging loudly enouf about going hither and thither through time like it was some fancy garden. Maybe they couldn't really do anything bout time and they would just kill us and not be able to unkill us. Maybe they could go back and unkill us and then they woulda killed us but we would be unkilt. Damn this time travel anyways, why didn't me and Tom justa stayed in the cave!

"Now you can see your time ship," Mr. Smith, the assassin said, "All of you are invited. We must make haste as time is awasting, which is a quaint phrase, given what we know of time, eh Mr. Smith."

Mr. Smith didn't say nothing, he just follered the assassin out the door as did Mr. Quatermain, Tom and I. Ise admit, I was concerned about getting kilt, Ise also admits that I don't think they was anything more confusin than my thoughts about being kilt and unkilt and how'd you know the difference even' it had happened to you and whether or not it had happened already to us and we just didn't remember cause the no goods had changed history. Most of all Ise admits I was some curious to see the time machine, as I had a hunch that regarldless of what the assassin thought, he hadn't reckoned on the brain power of Tom and Mr. Quatermain so the story warn't told yet by a long shot.

11

The Time Ship

The no goods did good by themselves even if they didn't by others. They had a warehouse that looked like any other big old wooden building you had ever seen , on the outside, but inside was some more pretty. It had lots of doo dads hither and yon on the walls and it was the hugest single place I had ever seen on the insides. They was about 8 of them no goods about including the assassin. They all had them silver guns, which was plenty dangerous but then again, I reckon if you is killed by a silver gun or by a black gun, or even a pink and purple gun, you was just as dead.

The four of us were sitting on the floor and not in chairs and I knows from experience that it's harder to get going when you aint' in a chair so I reckons even future people knows that trick. While I was none to happy being there, I ain't so sure about Tom, as he was a sitting, quite like, and that's general when he's most dangerous.

The time ship was off to the left of us and there were two of them bad guys with silver rifles standing in front of it, but the door to it was open.

"Now Mr. Smith," the assassin says, "It is time for you to answer a few of our questions, first and foremost being, where is the control knob for the time sphere."

"Why should I?" answered Mr. Smith, "As you have already told us we are marked for death. Please just get on with it and let's not waste words, as I will not help you, even if I could, as I too choose death before dishonor." Then I sees Mr. Smith do something funny with his mouth and he fell flat on his face.

The smell of burnt almonds came to my nose and I thought, I'se glad them things don't grow in Mizzou as they are powerful dangerous.

The assassin looks sheepish as one does when they's been out thunk, even if he was a gonna kill Mr. Smith hisself, he certainly wanted the honor of doing same, and didn't like he was beaten outta his game. The assassin walked over and bent down and not only smelt but felt Mr. Smith and came away, pretty much shore that Mr. Smith warn't playing possum but was definite dead.

"It appears I have overlooked the obvious," the assassin stated a bit lamely I thought, "Who would have thought he would have taken precautions such as this without knowing he was under scrutiny." The assassin rose, shrugged his shoulders and then said, "Well at least we have Mr. Quatermain."

The assassin, walked over to Mr. Quatermain and said, "Do I need to look inside your mouth?"

"You might not want to," Mr. Quatermain said, "As I did take the precaution of eating garlic before our meeting."

The assassin smiled, thou I didn't cause I didn't know what garlic was but I figured it was something stanky.

"That will not protect you, Mr. Quatermain," the assassin said ominously. "We will be off to another room, if you do not mind, as we have much to discuss, and some of our words may not be fit for the ears of the young."

The assassin may'uv thought he was doin me and Tom a favor, but I'se got to admit, if they's a cuss word that a boy ain't heard by the time he's 12, then it ain't worth knowing.

One of them other no goods, points his gun at me and Tom and says, "This way gentlemen," which is how they's talk instead a saying, "Get on over there," which is what he meant.

Tom and I turned and was walking towards the way he pointed when Tom says to me real quite like, "Huck, close your eyes and get ready for some doings," which I was a ready for any sort of doings that would keep me from getting Kilt and suddenly we had doings aplenty.

Mr. Smith, rose from the dead and flung something on the floor that was bright as the sun. Tom grabbed me at that time, and he drug me to the floor, as the guys with the silver rifles was a shooting this way and that and they was hitting stuff and they was screaming and then there was a loud noise and the door we had come in through was flung open and there came Utumbo along with about a dozen men, with rifles that warn't silent and they was a shooting this a ways and that.

Tom then grabs me offen the floor and says "Let's go Huck, we need to get to the time machine and protect it from the assassin," which was a good sentiment, but how we could protect anything from someone with guns when we didn't have any was uncertain to me.

The bright light had faded and some of the men were getting some of their eyesight back. They were pot shotting left right and all about, aiming for Utempo and others. Mr. Quatermain and Mr. Smith was tangled up with a couple of the no goods, and they was a heaving lefts and rights at each other, and all a trying to get to the silver rifles that were scattered about the floor. The two men that had been guarding the time sphere was flat on the floor and they were bleeding from a couple of parts of their body.

As Tom and I jumped through the door, we saw the assassin headed our way. Tom reached into his pocket and pulled out a knob, "Mr. Smith gave me the control knob," he said, and "He and Quatermain, told me that I must ensure that the assassin does not get ahold of it."

"Then you's better do something," I said, "As that no good assassin, is just about here."

Now I still don't know what happened, and whether it was accident or just Tom being Tom, but he screwed that knob onto the post and he pushed the lever that was on the post. Then we weren't there anymore, which is a hard thing to explain, but it was true. We was still in the time sphere, but the time sphere warn't in the warehouse anymore, but just in an open lot as I had discovered when Tom told me with a quite voice, "Open the door Huck and be prepared to swing and duck at the same time, in case the assassin or one of them no goods are there."

As I opened the door and saw that we were just out in the open, and I turned and says to Tom in a rising voice "Tom,I shore do hope you knows what's you is doing, as I don't know where we is are how we got here."

"Well we are somewhere else in time," Tom said, and he said it with no more emotion than saying we was late for school.

Tom unscrewed the control knob and put it back into his pocket, and then began to explain what had happened. "Mr. Quatermain and Mr. Smith had talked to me about their plans to regain this time ship," Tom the explainer, explained, "And we all agreed that the assassin would likely not talk. We agreed the only way to discover the time ship was to have ourselves taken to it, and then to depend on Mr. Quatrmain's team to come in and rescue us. Mr. Smith had a drug that would make him appear dead but would only make him appear dead for a few minutes, just long enough to fool the assassin. Therefore, we agreed that at the right moment, he would act out his fake suicide and then he would come awake and throw that light bomb to hide our actions. We thought at a minimum we would all make the time ship and we could go on our ways, of course, we did not know that Utumbo would come in at the worst possible time to save us and that there would be a lot of activity going on that would keep Mr. Quatermain and Mr. Smith from getting to the time ship, but even so, I had to get the ship away from them No Goods."

"Well Tom, " I said, " I am powerful happy that we didn't get killed, but I don't know that we have done anything to brag about, as the assassin will just take his own time ship and go back and get us again, or somen like that, as it is too damn hard for me to think on, but thinks on it I does."

"But don't you see Huck," Tom replied, "The assassin, can't have another time ship, or he wouldn't have allowed us to capture him anyway as he would have just gone back in time and not been pushed in the bay to start with." Lessen this was the first time, I thought, but I didn't say anything. "So what

Mr. smith thought was that there is only one time ship, his, and that the assassin, had brought back that time ship and his ancestor had gotten aholdt of it, and all of this is playing out as it should. In other words, this time ship, will be the one that his ancestor builds and there is only the one ship and he will park it somewhere in time and the assassin will find it and come back in time and that's how he got here, but then lost track of it and then Mr. smith finds it and then he comes back in time and he finds the assassin who lost it in the first place and …."

"Tom," I says as I hold up my hand and says, "Let's just say they's only the one ship and we is in it and leave out the whys and wherefores, as it is morn' a might confusing, so I will sure take your word on it." I gotta admit that what Tom was saying didn't just natural follow, but then Tom is just smarter than I, and I gave it up as a mystery much as predestiny and why girls exist.

"Might better," Tom agreed and he said, "We've got to find out when we are," which is a strange thing to hear as you typically asks where are we, "So that we can determine how to go back in time and help Mr. Quatermain and Mr. Smith and to prevent the Brotherood from having control of the time ship and…"

"Please, Tom", I said, "Please don't chase that monkey around the mulberry tree no more, as I am not just a bit confused and have a headaches and, though I don't want to seem ungrateful for you saving my life, I do so want to quit thinking in circles for awhiles."

Out we walked into London England, as the time ship moves through time but not through space, at least Mr. Smith would have it so and I had no reason to disbelieve him. There were shops a plenty up and down the street and Tom said "Let's get a newspaper and find out the date," which made as much sense as anything else I'd heard.

At the end of the street we was walking was a newsstand and that's where we walked. A young'un was a screaming out some head line or other that I paid no mind to and Tom just looked at the paper, and didn't try to buy it, which caused the newspaper seller to say "Get lost ladies, or pony up some hapennies for that paper."

Tom just smiled and said , "I have what I need mister, keep your paper."

Tom and I walked slightly away from the newspaper stand and Tom says, "It is March 14, 1837. Now that I know the date, I should be able to figure out how to get the time machine back to an appropriate time to protect Mr. smith and Mr. Quatermain."

"I hopes so, " I replied, and I did hope so, because, they aint nothing about any of this incident that makes a whole lotta sense to the uneducated. As we walked back towards the time ship, we were sudden like bumped into by a couple of youngsters. One of them was at least Tom's age but the other was young and didn't look morn ten. They hit us, and it looked like an accident, but me being the one that had used this technique before hollered out "Whole on to your stuff Tom, as these are pickpockets."

Neither Tom or I are babes in the woods when it comes to boys being thieves, but me of course much morn' Tom, as Pap wanted me to have a perfession after he was gone and he thought pick pocketing was a good as any. Still, these boys were something to behold and I gotta say that their technique was something to behold. I'se never seen any human that quick and nimble and they had Tom's wallet in a heartbeat and they was running off.

"Let's get em, Huck," Tom shouted and that's what we tried to do, but even tho we was faster, we didn't know them back alleys and fences the way that they did and it didn't take them morn' five minutes to shake us.

"Well Tom, I guess we's broke," but it diidn't bother me oversome as I'd been broke most of my life and I had survived.

"It's worse than that, Huck, much worse," and Tom said in the saddest voice I had ever heard on this here green earth "They got the control knob to the time sphere, and we can't do anything about Mr. Quatermain and Mr. Smith until we get it back."

Tom and I walked dejected like back to the newsstand and we saw the young un still screaming out the days news. Tom knows that lotsa boys knows each other when they's in the same general area so he thought maybe the young un would know who they were, so he says, "Hey young feller, do you know who that was that accosted us?"

The young un looked back and said, "If accosted means stole your stuff Guvner I surely do, you have the particular honor of being robbed by the best pick pocket in all of London, and likely all of the world. We calls him the Artful Dodger."

www.ingramcontent.com/pod-product-compliance
Lightning Source LLC
Chambersburg PA
CBHW022039170626
46808CB00003B/1271